The guy with the eyes stood up, and everybody in the joint shut up and turned to look at him.

He was unreasonably tall, near seven foot, dressed in a black suit that fit worse than a Joliet Special, and his shoes didn't look right either. After a moment you realized that he had the left shoe on the right foot, and vice versa, but it didn't surprise you. He was thin and deeply tanned and his mouth was twisted up tight but mostly he was eyes, and I still dream of those eyes and wake up sweating now and again. They were like windows into hell, the very personal and private hell of a man faced with a dilemma he cannot resolve . . .

And when he sadly confessed that he was sent by an alien race to destroy the earth, no one in the place was surprised. Hell, *anything* can happen at Callahan's.

CALLAHAN'S CROSSTIME SALOON

"Robinson is the hottest writer to hit SF since Ellison, and he can match the master's frenetic energy and emotional intensity, arm-break for gut-wrench."

—*Los Angeles Times*

Berkley Books by Spider Robinson

CALLAHAN'S CROSSTIME SALOON
CALLAHAN'S SECRET
MINDKILLER
NIGHT OF POWER

CALLAHAN'S CROSSTIME SALOON

SPIDER ROBINSON

BERKLEY BOOKS, NEW YORK

Parts of this book were previously published in *Analog* and *Vertex*.

All characters in this book are fictitious.
Any resemblance to actual persons, living or dead,
is purely coincidental.

CALLAHAN'S CROSSTIME SALOON

A Berkley Book / published by arrangement with
the author

PRINTING HISTORY
Ace Science Fiction edition / June 1977
Eighth printing / June 1984
Berkley edition / January 1987

ISBN: 0-425-09586-X

A BERKLEY BOOK ® TM 757,375
Berkley Books are published by The Berkley Publishing Group,
200 Madison Avenue, New York, New York 10016.
The name "BERKLEY" and the stylized "B" with design
are trademarks belonging to Berkley Publishing Corporation.

PRINTED IN THE UNITED STATES OF AMERICA

To Ben Bova

CONTENTS

Spider Robinson:
The SF Writer As Empath

By Ben Bova

When *Analog* magazine was housed over at Graybar Building on Lexington Avenue, our offices were far from plush. In fact, they were grimy. Years worth of Manhattan soot clung to the walls. The windows were opaque with grime. (What has this to do with Spider Robinson? Patience, friend.)

Many times young science fiction fans would come to Manhattan and phone me from Grand Central Station, which connected underground with the good old Graybar. "I've just come to New York and I read every issue of *Analog* and I'd like to come up and see what a science fiction magazine office looks like," they would invariably say.

I'd tell them to come on up, but not to expect too much. My advice was always ignored. The poor kid would come in and gape at the piles of manuscripts, the battered old metal desks, and mountains of magazines and stacks of artwork, the ramshackle filing cabinets and bookshelves. His eyes would fill with tears. His mouth would sag open.

He had, of course, expected whirring computers, telephones with TV attachments, smoothly efficient robots humming away, ultramodern furniture, and a general appearance reminiscent of a NASA clean room. (Our present offices, in the spanking new Condé Nast Building on Madison Avenue, are a little closer to that dream.)

The kid would shamble away, heartsick, the beautiful

rainbow-hued bubble of his imagination burst by the sharp prick of reality.

Still, despite the cramped quarters and the general dinginess, we managed to put out an issue of *Analog* each month, and more readers bought it than any other science fiction book, magazine, pamphlet, or cuneiform tablet ever published.

And then came Spider Robinson.

Truth to tell, I don't remember if he sent in a manuscript through the mail first, or telephoned for an appointment to visit the office. No matter. And now he's off in Nova Scotia, living among the stunted trees and frost heaves, where nobody—not even short-memoried editors—can reach him easily.

Anyway, in comes Spider. I look up from my desk and see this lank, almost-cadaverous young man, bearded, long of hair, slightly owlish behind his eyeglasses, sort of grinning quizzically, as if he didn't know what to expect. Neither did I.

But I thought, *At least he won't be put off by the interior decor.*

You have to understand that those same kids who expected *Analog*'s office to look like an out-take from *2001: A Space Odyssey* also had a firm idea of what an *Analog* writer should look like: a tall, broadshouldered, jutjawed, steelyeyed hero who can repair a starship's inertial drive with one hand, make friends with the fourteen-legged green aliens of Arcturus, and bring the warring nations of Earth together under a benignly scientific world government—all at the same time, while wearing a metallic mesh jumpsuit and a cool smile.

Never mind that no SF writer ever looked like that. Well, maybe Robert A. Heinlein comes close, and he could certainly do all of those things if he'd just stop writing for a while. But Asimov is a bit less than heroic in stature; Silverberg shuns politics; Bradbury doesn't even drive a car, much less a starship.

Nevertheless, this was the popular conception of a typical *Analog* writer. Spider Robinson was rather wider of that mark than most.

He had a story with him, called "The Guy with the Eyes." There wasn't much science fiction in it. But it was one helluva good story. About a crazy bunch of guys who get together at a truly unique place called Callahan's.

We went to lunch, and Spider began telling me how he worked nights guarding a sewer 'way out on Long Island. Far from being a drop-out, he was writing stories and songs, as well as sewer-sitting. He's a worker, and he knows science fiction very well, a fact that surprised a lot of people when he started reviewing books for *Galaxy* magazine. He's also a guitar-strummin' singer, and I found out how good he is at many a party. But that was later.

I bought "The Guy with the Eyes." When it came out in *Analog*, it caused a mild ripple among our readers. I had expected some of them to complain because it wasn't galaxy-spanning superheroic science fiction. Instead, they wrote to tell me that they got a kick out of Callahan's Place. How about more of the same?

Now, an editor spends most of his time reading lousy stories. John Campbell, who ran *Analog* (née *Astounding*) for some thirty-five years, often claimed to hold the Guinness Book of Records championship for reading more rotten SF stories than anyone else on Earth. (Most likely he could have expanded his claim to take in the entire solar system, but John was a conservative man in some ways.)

So when you spend your days and nights—especially the nights—reading poor stories, it's a pleasure to run across somebody like Spider: a new writer who has a good story to tell. It makes all those lousy stories worthwhile. Almost.

It's a thrill to get a good story out of the week's slushpile—that mountain of manuscripts sent in by the unknowns, the hopefuls, the ones who want to be writers but haven't written anything publishable yet.

But the *real* thrill comes when a new writer sends in his second story and it's even better than the first one. That happens most rarely of all. It happened with Spider. He brought in the manuscript of "The Time Traveler," and I knew I was dealing with a pro, not merely a one-time amateur.

We talked over the story before he completed the writing of it. He warned me that he couldn't really find a science fiction gimmick to put into the story. I fretted over that (*Analog* is, after all, a science fiction magazine), but then I realized that the protagonist was indeed a time traveller; his "time machine" was a prison.

Just about the time the story was published, thousands of similar time travelers returned to the U.S. from North Vietnamese prisons. Spider's story should have been required reading for all of them, and their families.

Sure enough, we got a few grumbles from some of our older readers. One sent a stiff note, saying that since the story wasn't science fiction atall, and he was paying for science fiction stories, would we please cancel his subscription. I wrote him back pointing out that we had published the best science fiction stories in the world for more than forty years, and for one single story he's cancelling his subscription? He never responded, and I presume that he's been happy with *Analog* and Spider ever since.

Callahan's Place grew to be an institution among *Analog*'s readers, and you can see it—and the zanies who frequent Callahan's—in all their glory in this collection of stories. What you're reading is something truly unique, because the man who wrote these stories is an unique writer. It's been my privilege to publish most of these stories in *Analog*. Several others are brand new and haven't been published anywhere else before.

It's also been a privilege, and a helluva lot of fun, to get to know Spider personally. To watch him develop as a writer and as a man.

He went from guarding sewers to working for a Long Island newspaper. When that job brought him to a crisis of conscience—work for the paper and slant the news the way the publisher demanded, or get out—his conscience won. He took the big, big step of depending on nothing but his writing talent for an income. But Spider *writes*; he doesn't talk about writing, he works at it.

It wasn't all that easy. He had personal problems, just like everybody else does. Not every story he put on paper sold immediately. Money was always short.

One summer afternoon he met a girlfriend who was coming into town from Nova Scotia. She had never been to New York before. Spider greeted her at Penn Station with the news that his lung had just collapsed and he had to get to a hospital right away, he hoped she didn't mind. The young lady (her name is Jeanne) not only got him to a hospital; she ended up marrying him. Now they both live in Nova Scotia, where city-born Spider has found that he loves the rural splendor of farm life. (Me, I stay in the wilds of Manhattan, where all you've got to worry about is strikes, default, muggings and equipment failure. Nova Scotia? In winter? Ugh!)

Meanwhile, Spider's stories kept getting better. He branched out from Callahan's. He turned a ludicrous incident on a Greyhound bus into a fine and funny science fiction story. He wrote a novel with so many unlikely angles to it that if I gave you the outline of it, it would probably drive you temporarily insane. But he made it work. It's a damned good novel, with bite as well as humanity in it. We'll publish a big slice of it in *Analog*, and it will come out both in hardcover and paperback later on.

And his stories were being noticed, appreciated, enjoyed by the science fiction fans. At the World Science Fiction Convention in 1974 he received the John Campbell Award as Best New Writer of the Year. At that time he had only published three or four stories, but they were not the kind that could be overlooked.

What does it all add up to? Here we have a young writer who looks, at first glance, like the archetypical hippie dropout, winning respect and admiration in a field that's supposed to admire nobody but the Heinleins and Asimovs.

It just might be that Spider Robinson represents the newest and strongest trend in science fiction today. He's a humanist, by damn. An empath. He's sensitive to human emotions: pain, fear, joy, love. He can get them down on paper as few writers can.

The SF field began with gadgeteers and pseudoscience. It developed in the Thirties and Forties with writers such as Heinlein and Asimov, who knew and understood real science and engineering, and could write strong stories about believable people who were scientists and engineers. In the Fifties and Sixties we began to get voices such as Ted Sturgeon, Fred Pohl, Harlan Ellison—writers who warned that not everything coming from the laboratory was Good, True and Beautiful.

Now here's Spider Robinson, writing stories that are—well, they're about *people*. People in pain, people having fun, people with problems, people helping each other to solve their problems. Spider is a guy who can feel other people's emotions and help to deal with them. He's like a character out of an early Sturgeon story—kind, down-to-earth, very empathic. Literarily, he is Sturgeon's heir.

That's the good news. He is also an inveterate punster. You'll see his puns scattered all through the Callahan stories. In fact, there are whole evenings at Callahan's devoted to punning contests. Nobody's perfect.

I remember getting a newspaper clipping from Spider which showed a NASA drawing of the design for a toilet to be used under zero gravity conditions in the Skylab satellite. (NASA has problems that thee and me can't even guess at.) The cutaway drawing of this engineering marvel showed that there was a rotating blade inside the toilet bowl, to ''separate the liquid from the solid wastes,'' as NASA's engineers euphemistically put it.

Spider, in his scrawly handwriting, had scribbled across the top of the clipping a brief note, followed by an arrow that pointed unerringly to the bowl and the separator blade. The note said, ''Ben: Near as I can figure, the shit is *supposed* to hit the fan!''

As I said, nobody's perfect. But Spider comes pretty damned close. Read about him and his friends at Callahan's Place. Enjoy.

April, 1976
New York City

Foreword
by Spider Robinson

Books get written for the damndest reasons. Some are written to pay off a mortgage, some to save the world, some simply for lack of anything better to do. One of my favorite anecdotes concerns a writer who bet a friend that it was literally impossible to write a book so B*A*D that no one could be found to publish it. As the story goes, this writer proceeded to write the worst, most hackneyed novel of which he was capable—and not only did he succeed in selling it, *the public demanded better than two dozen sequels* (I *can't* tell you his name: his estate might sue, and I have no documentation. Ask around at any SF convention; it's a reasonably famous anecdote).

This book, as it happens, was begun for the single purpose of getting me out of the sewer.

I mean that literally. In 1971, after *seven years* in college, with that Magic Piece of Paper clutched triumphantly in my fist, the best job I was able to get was night watchman on a sewer project in Babylon, New York —guarding a hole in the ground to prevent anyone from stealing it. God *bless* the American educational system.

What with one thing and another, I seemed to have a lot of time on my hands. So I read a lot of science fiction, a custom I have practiced assiduously since, at the age of five, I was introduced to Robert A. Heinlein's *Rocket Ship Galileo*. One evening, halfway through a particularly wretched example of Sturgeon's Law ("Ninety percent of science fiction—of *anything*—is crap"), I sat up straight in my chair and said for perhaps the ten thousandth time in my life, "By Jesus, *I* can write better than this turnip."

And a lightbulb of about two hundred watts appeared in the air over my head.

I had written a couple of stories already, acquiring just enough rejection slips to impress friends with, and had actually had one printed in a now-defunct fanzine called *Xrymph*. (Hilariously enough, one of the crazies who produced *Xrymph* was the editor who bought this book that you hold in your hands: Jim Frenkel.) But my entire output at that time could have been fit into a business envelope, and its quality might be most charitably described as shitful. On the other hand, I had never before had the motivation I now possessed: I Wanted Out Of The Sewer.

It was time to become a Pro.

I realized from previous failures that as a tyro, it behooved me to select a subject I knew thoroughly, as I was not yet skillful enough to bluff convincingly. Accordingly, I selected drink. Within a week I had completed the first chapter of this book, "The Guy With The Eyes."

Looking in a library copy of *Writer's Guide*, I discovered that there were four markets for my masterpiece. I noted that Ben Bova paid five cents a word and everyone else paid under three, and that's how my lifelong friendship with Ben was begun. I mailed it and he bought it, and when I had recovered from the shock of his letter of acceptance, I gathered my nerve and rang him up to timidly ask if editors ever condescended to waste a few minutes answering the naive questions of beginning writers. Ben pointed out that without writers, editors couldn't exist, and invited me to lunch. And when I walked into the *Analog* office (stumbling over the occasional Hugo), very nearly the first thing he said was, "Say, does that Callahan's Place really *exist*? I'd *love* to go there."

Since that day I estimate I have been asked that question about $5,372 \times 10^{10}$ times, by virtually every fan I meet. One gentleman wrote to me complaining bitterly because I had said in "The Guy With The Eyes" that Callahan's was in Suffolk County, Long Island, and he wanted me to know that he had by God spent six months combing every single bar on Long Island without finding the Place.

I seem to have struck a chord.

Well I'm sorry, but I'll have to tell you the same thing I told those $5,372 \times 10^{10}$ other people: as far as I know, Callahan's Place exists only between a) my ears, b) assorted *Analog* and *Vertex* covers, and of course c) the covers of this book. If there is in fact a Callahan's Place out there in the so-called real world, and you know where it is, I sincerely hope *you'll* tell *me*.

'Cause I'd really like to hang out there awhile.

February, 1976
Phinney's Cove, Nova Scotia

"There is nothing which has been contrived by man by which so much happiness has been produced as by a good tavern or inn."

—Samuel Johnson

1

The Guy With The Eyes

Callahan's Place was pretty lively that night. Talk fought Budweiser for mouth space all over the joint, and the beer nuts supply was critical. But this guy managed to keep himself in a corner without being noticed for nearly an hour. I only spotted him myself a few minutes before all the action started, and I make a point of studying *everybody* at Callahan's Place.

First thing, I saw those eyes. You get used to some haunted eyes in Callahan's—the newcomers have 'em —but these reminded me of a guy I knew once in Topeka, who got four people with an antique revolver before they cut him down.

I hoped like hell he'd visit the fireplace before he left.

If you've never been to Callahan's Place, God's pity on you. Seek it in the wilds of Suffolk County, but look not for neon. A simple, hand-lettered sign illuminated by a single floodlight, and a heavy oaken door split in the center (by the head of one Big Beef McCaffrey in 1947) and poorly repaired.

Inside, several heresies.

First, the light is about as bright as you keep your living room. Callahan maintains that people who like to drink in caves are unstable.

1

Second, there's a flat rate. Every drink in the house is half a buck, with the option. The option operates as follows:

You place a one-dollar bill on the bar. If all you have on you is a fin, you trot across the street to the all-night deli, get change, come back and put a one-dollar bill on the bar. (Callahan maintains that nobody in his right mind would counterfeit one-dollar bills; most of us figure he just likes to rub fistfuls of them across his face after closing.)

You are served your poison-of-choice. You inhale this, and confront the option. You may, as you leave, pick up two quarters from the always-full cigarbox at the end of the bar and exit into the night. Or you may, upon finishing your drink, stride up to the chalk line in the middle of the room, announce a toast (this is mandatory) and hurl your glass into the huge, oldfashioned fireplace which takes up most of the back wall. You then depart without visiting the cigarbox. Or, pony up another buck and exercise your option again.

Callahan seldom has to replenish the cigarbox. He orders glasses in such quantities that they cost him next to nothing, and he sweeps out the fireplace himself every morning.

Another heresy: no one watches you with accusing eyes to make sure you take no more quarters than you have coming to you. If Callahan ever happens to catch someone cheating him, he personally ejects them forever. Sometimes he doesn't open the door first. The last time he had to eject someone was in 1947, a gentleman named Big Beef McCaffrey.

Not too surprisingly, it's a damned interesting place to be. It's the kind of place you hear about only if you need to—and if you are very lucky. Because if a patron, having proposed his toast and smithereened his glass, feels like talking about the nature of his troubles, he receives the instant, undivided attention of everyone in the room.

(That's why the toast is obligatory. Many a man with a hurt locked inside finds in the act of naming his hurt for the toast that he wants very much to talk about it. Callahan is one smart hombre.) On the other hand, even the most tantalizingly cryptic toast will bring no prying inquiries if the guy displays no desire to uncork. Anyone attempting to flout this custom is promptly blackjacked by Fast Eddie the piano player and dumped in the alley.

But somehow many do feel like spilling it in a place like Callahan's; and you can get a deeper insight into human nature in a week there than in ten years anywhere else I know. You can also quite likely find solace for most any kind of trouble, from Callahan himself if no one else. It's a rare hurt that can stand under the advice, help and sympathy generated by upwards of thirty people that *care*. Callahan loses a lot of his regulars. After they've been coming around long enough, they find they don't need to drink any more.

It's that kind of a bar.

I don't want you to get a picture of Callahan's Place as an agonized, Alcoholics Anonymous type of group-encounter session, with Callahan as some sort of salty psychoanalyst-father-figure in the foreground. Hell, many's the toast provokes roars of laughter, or a shouted chorus of agreement, or a unanimous blitz of glasses from all over the room when the night is particularly spirited. Callahan is tolerant of rannygazoo; he maintains that a bar should be "merry," so long as no bones are broken unintentionally. I mind the time he helped Spud Flynn set fire to a seat cushion to settle a bet on which way the draft was coming. Callahan exudes, at all times, a kind of monolithic calm; and u.s. 40 is shorter than his temper.

This night I'm telling you about, for instance, was nothing if not merry. When I pulled in around ten o'clock, there was an unholy shambles of a square dance going on in the middle of the floor. I laid a dollar on the bar, collected a glass of Tullamore Dew and a hello-grin from Callahan, and settled back in a tall chair—Callahan abhors barstools—to observe the goings-on. That's what I mean about Callahan's Place: most bars, men only dance if there're ladies around. Of one sex or another.

I picked some familiar faces out of the maelstrom of madmen weaving and lurching over honest-to-God sawdust, and waved a few greetings. There was Tom Flannery, who at that time had eight months to live, and knew it; he laughed a lot at Callahan's Place. There was Slippery Joe Maser, who had two wives, and Marty Matthias, who didn't gamble any more, and Noah Gonzalez, who worked on Suffolk County's bomb squad. Calling for the square dance while performing a creditable Irish jig was Doc Webster, fat and jovial as the day he pumped the pills out of my stomach and ordered me to Callahan's. See, I used to have a wife and daughter before I decided to install my own brakes. I saved thirty dollars, easy . . .

The Doc left the square-dancers to their fate—their creative individuality making a caller superfluous—and drifted over like a pink zeppelin to say Hello. His stethoscope hung unnoticed from his ears, framing a smile like a sunlamp. The end of the 'scope was in his drink.

"Howdy, Doc. Always wondered how you kept that damned thing so cold," I greeted him.

He blinked like an owl with the staggers and looked down at the gently bubbling pickup beneath two fingers of scotch. Emitting a bellow of laughter at about force eight, he removed the gleaming thing and shook it experimentally.

"My secret's out, Jake. Keep it under your hat, will you?" he boomed.

"Maybe you better keep it under yours," I suggested. He appeared to consider this idea for a time, while I speculated on one of life's greatest paradoxes: Sam Webster, M.D. The Doc is good for a couple of quarts of Peter Dawson a night, three or four nights a week. But you won't find a better sawbones anywhere on Earth, and those sausage fingers of his can move like a tap-dancing centipede when they have to, with nary a tremor. Ask Shorty Steinitz to tell you about the time Doc Webster took out his appendix on top of Callahan's bar . . . while Callahan calmly kept the Scotch coming.

"At least then I could hear myself think," the Doc finally replied, and several people seated within earshot groaned theatrically.

"Have a heart, Doc," one called out.

"What a re-pulse-ive idea," the Doc returned the serve.

"Well, I know when I'm beat," said the challenger, and made as if to turn away.

"Why, you young whelp, aorta poke you one," roared the Doc, and the bar exploded with laughter and cheers. Callahan picked up a beer bottle in his huge hand and pegged it across the bar at the Doc's round skull. The beer bottle, being made of foam rubber, bounced gracefully into the air and landed in the piano, where Fast Eddie sat locked in mortal combat with the "C-Jam Blues."

Fast Eddie emitted a sound like an outraged transmission and kept right on playing, though his upper register was shot. "Little beer never hoit a piano," he sang out as he reached the bridge, and went over it like he figured to burn it behind him.

All in all it looked like a cheerful night, but then I saw the Janssen kid come in and I knew there was a trouble brewing.

This Janssen kid—look, I can't knock long hair, I wore mine long when it wasn't fashionable. And I can't knock pot for the same reason. But nobody I know ever had a good thing to say for heroin. Certainly not Joe Hennessy, who did two weeks in the hospital last year after he surprised the Janssen kid scooping junk-money ou of his safe at four in the morning. Old Man Janssen paid Hennessy back every dime and disowned the kid, and he'd been in and out of sight ever since. Word was he was still using the stuff, but the cops never seemed to catch him holding. They sure did try, though. I wondered what the hell he was doing in Callahan's Place.

I should know better by now. He placed a tattered bill on the bar, took the shot of bourbon which Callahan handed him silently, and walked to the chalk line. He was quivering with repressed tension, and his boots squeaked on the sawdust. The place quieted down some, and his toast—"To smack!"—rang out clear and crisp. Then he downed the shot amid an expanding silence and flung his glass so hard you could hear his shoulder crack just before the glass shattered on unyielding brick.

Having created silence, he broke it. With a sob. Even as he let it out he glared around to see what our reactions were.

Callahan's was immediate, an "Amen!" that sounded like an echo of the smashing glass. The kid made a face like he was somehow satisfied in spite of himself, and looked at the rest of us. His gaze rested on Doc Webster, and the Doc drifted over and gently began rolling up the kid's sleeves. The boy made no effort to help or hinder him. When they were both rolled to the shoulder—phosporescent purple I think they were—he silently held out his arms, palm-up.

They were absolutely unmarked. Skinny as hell and white as a piece of paper, but unmarked. The kid was clean.

Everyone waited in silence, giving the kid their respectful attention. It was a new feeling to him, and he didn't quite know how to handle it. Finally he said, "I heard about this place," just a little too truculently.

"Then you must of needed to," Callahan told him quietly, and the kid nodded slowly.

"I hear you get some answers in, from time to time," he half-asked.

"Now and again," Callahan admitted. "Some o' the damndest questions, too. What's it like, for instance?"

"You mean smack?"

"I don't mean bourbon."

The kid's eyes got a funny, far-away look, and he almost smiled. "It's . . ." He paused, considering. "It's like . . . being dead."

"Whooee!" came a voice from across the room. "That's a powerful good feeling indeed." I looked and saw it was Chuck Samms talking, and watched to see how the kid would take it.

He thought Chuck was being sarcastic and snapped back, "Well, what the hell do you know about it anyway?" Chuck smiled. A lot of people ask him that question, in a different tone of voice.

"Me?" he said, enjoying himself hugely. "Why, I've been dead is all."

"S'truth," Callahan confirmed as the kid's jaw dropped. "Chuck there was legally dead for five minutes before the Doc got his pacemaker going again. The crumb died owing me money, and I never had the heart to dun his widow."

"Sure was a nice feeling, too," Chuck said around a yawn. "More peaceful than nap-time in a monastery. If it wasn't so pleasant I wouldn't be near so damned scared of it." There was an edge to his voice as he finished, but it disappeared as he added softly, "What the hell would you want to be dead for?"

The Janssen kid couldn't meet his eyes, and when he spoke his voice cracked. "Like you said, pop, peace. A little peace of mind, a little quiet. Nobody yammering at you all the time. I mean, if you're dead there's always the chance somebody'll mourn, right? Make friends with the worms, dig *their* side of it, maybe a little poltergeist action, who knows? I mean, what's the sense of talking about it, anyway? Didn't any of you guys ever just want to run away?''

"Sure thing," said Callahan. "Sometimes I do it too. But I generally run someplace I can find my way back from.'' It was said so gently that the kid couldn't take offense, though he tried.

"Run away from what, son?" asked Slippery Joe.

The kid had been bottled up tight too long; he exploded. "From what?" he yelled. "Jesus, where do I start? There was this war they wanted me to go and fight, see? And there's this place called college, I mean they want you to care, dig it, care about this education trip, and they don't care enough themselves to make it as attractive as the crap game across the street. There's this air I hear is unfit to breathe, and water that ain't fit to drink, and food that wouldn't nourish a vulture and a grand outlook for the future. You can't get to a job without the car you couldn't afford to run even if you were working, and if you *found* a job it'd pay five dollars less than the rent. The T.V. advertises karate classes for four-year-olds and up, the President's New Clothes didn't wear very well, the next depression's around the corner and you ask me what in the name of God I'm running from?

"Man, I've been straight for seven months, what I mean, and in that seven god damned months I have been over this island like a fungus and there is *nothing* for me. No jobs, no friends, no place to live long enough to get the floor dirty, no money and nobody that doesn't point and say "Junkie" when I go by for seven *months* and you ask me what am I running from? Man, *everything* is all, just everything.''

It was right then that I noticed that guy in the corner, the one with the eyes. Remember him? He was leaning forward in rapt attention, his mouth a black slash in a face pulled tight as a drumhead. Those ghastly eyes of his never left the Janssen kid, but somehow I was sure that his awareness included all of us, everyone in the room.

And no one had an answer for the Janssen boy. I could see, all around the room, men who had learned to *listen* Callahan's Place, men who had learned to empathize, to want to understand and share the pain of another. And no one had a word to say. They were thinking past the blurted words of a haunted boy, wondering if this crazy world of confusion might not after all be one holy hell of a place to grow up. Most of them already had reason to know damn well that society never forgives the sinner, but they were realizing to their dismay how thin and uncomforting the straight and narrow has become these last few years.

Sure, they'd heard these things before, often enough to make them into clichés. But now I could see the boys reflecting that these were the clichés that made a young man say he liked to feel dead, and the same thought was mirrored on the face of each of them: *My God, when did we let these things become clichés?* The Problems of Today's Youth were no longer a Sunday supplement or a news broadcast or anything so remote and intangible, they were suddenly become a dirty, shivering boy who told us that in this world we had built for him with our sweat and our blood he was not only tired of living, but so *un*scared of dying that he did it daily, sometimes, for recreation.

And silence held court in Callahan's Place. No one had a single thing to say, and that guy with the eyes seemed to know it, and to derive some crazy kind of bitter inner satisfaction from the knowledge. He started to settle back in his chair, when Callahan broke the silence.

"So run," he said.

Just like that, flat, no expression, just, "So run." It hung there for about ten seconds, while he and the kid locked eyes.

The kid's forehead started to bead with sweat. Slowly, with shaking fingers, he reached under his leather vest to his shirt pocket. Knuckles white, he hauled out a flat, shiny black case about four inches by two. His eyes never left Callahan's as he opened it and held it up so that we could all see the gleaming hypodermic. It didn't look like it had ever been used; he must have just stolen it.

He held it up to the light for a moment, looking up his bare, unmarked arm at it, and then he whirled and flung it case and all into the giant fireplace. Almost as it shattered he sent a cellophane bag of white powder after it, and the powder burned green while the sudden stillness hung in the air. The guy with the eyes looked oddly stricken in some interior way, and he sat absolutely rigid in his seat.

And Callahan was around the bar in an instant, handing the Janssen kid a beer that grew out of his fist and roaring, "Welcome home, Tommy!" and no one in the place was very startled to realize that only Callahan of all of us knew the kid's first name.

We all sort of swarmed around then and swatted the kid on the arm some and he even cried a little until we poured some beer over his head and pretty soon it began to look like the night was going to get merry again after all.

And that's when the guy with the eyes stood up, and everybody in the joint shut up and turned to look at him. That sounds melodramatic, but it's the effect he had on us. When he moved, he was the center of attention. He was tall, unreasonably tall, near seven foot, and I'll never know why we hadn't all noticed him right off. He was dressed in a black suit that fit worse than a Joliet Special, and his shoes didn't look right either. After a moment you realized that he had the left shoe on the right foot, and vice-versa, but it didn't surprise you. He was thin and deeply tanned and his mouth was twisted up tight but mostly he was eyes, and I still dream of those eyes and wake up sweating now and again. They were like windows into hell, the very personal and private hell of a man faced with a dilemma he cannot resolve. They did not blink, not once.

He shambled to the bar, and something was wrong with his walk, too, like he was walking sideways on the wall with magnetic shoes and hadn't quite caught the knack yet. He took ten new singles out of his jacket pocket —which struck me as an odd place to keep cash—and laid them on the bar.

Callahan seemed to come back from a far place, and hustled around behind the bar again. He looked the stranger up and down and then placed ten shot glasses on the counter. He filled each with rye and stood back silently, running a big red hand through his thinning hair and regarding the stranger with clinical interest.

The dark giant tossed off the first shot, shuffled to the chalk line, and said in oddly-accented English, "To my profession," and hurled the glass into the fireplace.

Then he walked back to the bar and repeated the entire procedure. Ten times.

By the last glass, brick was chipping in the fireplace.

When the last, "To my profession," echoed in empty air, he turned and faced us. He waited, tensely, for question or challenge. There was none. He half turned away, paused, then swung back and took a couple of deep breaths. When he spoke his voice made you hurt to hear it.

"My profession, gentlemen," he said with that funny accent I couldn't place, "is that of advance scout. For a race whose home is many light-years from here. Many, many light-years from here." He paused, looking for our reactions.

Well, I thought, *ten whiskeys and he's a Martian.*

Indeed. Pleased to meet you, I'm Popeye the Sailor. I guess it was pretty obvious we were all thinking the same way, because he looked tired and said, "It would take far more ethanol than that to befuddle me, gentlemen." Nobody said a word to that, and he turned to Callahan. "You know I am not intoxicated," he stated.

Callahan considered him professionally and said finally, "Nope. You're not tight. I'll be a son of a bitch, but you're not tight."

The stranger nodded thanks, spoke thereafter directly to Callahan. "I am here now three days. In two hours I shall be finished. When I am finished I shall go home. After I have gone your planet will be vaporized. I have accumulated data which will ensure the annihilation of your species when they are assimilated by my Masters. To them, you will seem as cancerous cells, in danger of infecting all you touch. You will not be permitted to exist. You will be *cured*. And I repent me of my profession."

Maybe I wouldn't have believed it anywhere else. But at Callahan's Place *anything* can happen. Hell, we all believed him. Fast Eddie sang out, "Anyt'ing we can do about it?" and he was serious for sure. You can tell with Fast Eddie.

"I am helpless," the giant alien said dispassionately. "I contain . . . installations . . . which are beyond my influencing—or yours. They have recorded all the data I have perceived in these three days; in two hours a preset mechanism will be triggered and will transmit their contents to the Masters." I looked at my watch: it was eleven-fifteen. "The conclusions of the Masters are foregone. I cannot prevent the transmission; I cannot even attempt to. I am counterprogrammed."

"Why are you in this line of work if it bugs you so much?" Callahan wanted to know. No hostility, no panic. He was trying to *understand*.

"I am accustomed to take pride in my work," the alien

said. "I make safe the paths of the Masters. They must not be threatened by warlike species. I go before, to identify danger, and see to its neutralization. It is a good profession, I think. I thought."

"What changed your mind?" asked Doc Webster sympathetically.

"This place, this . . . 'bar' place we are in—this is not like the rest I have seen. Outside are hatred, competition, morals elevated to the status of ethics, prejudices elevated to the status of morals, whims elevated to the status of prejudices, all things with which I am wearily familiar, the classic symptoms of disease.

"But here is difference. Here in this place I sense qualities, attributes I did not know your species possessed, attributes which everywhere else in the known universe are mutually exclusive of the things I have perceived here tonight. They are good things . . . they cause me great anguish for your passing. They fill me with hurt.

"Oh, that I might lay down my geas," he cried. "I did not know that you had love!"

In the echoing stillness, Callahan said simply, "Sure we do, son. It's mebbe spread a little thin these days, but we've got it all right. Sure would be a shame if it all went up in smoke." He looked down at the rye bottle he still held in his big hand, and absently drank off a couple ounces. "Any chance that your masters might feel the same way?"

"None. Even I can still see that you must be destroyed if the Masters are to be safe. But for the first time in some thousands of years, I regret my profession. I fear I can do no more."

"No way you can gum up the works?"

"None. So long as I am alive and conscious, the transmission will take place. I could not assemble the volition to stop it. I have said: I am counterprogrammed."

I saw Noah Gonzalez' expression soften, heard him say, "Geez, buddy, that's hard lines." A mumbled agreement rose, and Callahan nodded slowly.

"That's tough, brother. I wouldn't want to be in your shoes."

He looked at us with absolute astonishment, the hurt in those terrible eyes of his mixed now with bewilderment. Shorty handed him another drink and it was like he didn't know what to do with it.

"You tell us how much it will take, mister," Shorty said respectfully, "and we'll get you drunk."

The tall man with star-burned skin groaned from deep within himself and backed away until the fireplace contained him. He and the flames ignored each other, and no one found it surprising.

"What is your matter?" he cried. "Why are you not destroying me? You fools, you need only destroy me and you are saved. I am your judge. I am your jury. I will be your executioner."

"You didn't ask for the job," Shorty said gently. "It ain't your doing."

"But you do not understand! If my data are not transmitted, the Masters will assume my destruction and avoid this system forever. Only the equal or superior of a Master could overcome my defenses, but I *can* control *them*. I will not use them. Do you comprehend me? I will not activate my defenses—you can destroy me and save yourselves and your species, and I will not hinder you.

"Kill me!" he shrieked.

There was a long, long pause, maybe a second or two, and then Callahan pointed to the drink Shorty still held out and growled, "You better drink that, friend. You need it. Talkin' of killin' in my joint. Wash your mouth out with bourbon and get outta that fireplace, I want to use it."

"Yeah, me too!" came the cry on all sides, and the big guy looked like he was gonna cry. Conversations started up again and Fast Eddie began playing "I Don't Want to Set the World On Fire," in very bad taste indeed.

Some of the boys wandered thoughtfully out, going home to tell their families, or settle their affairs. The rest of us, lacking either concern, drifted over to console the alien. I mean, where else would I want to be on Judgement Day?

He was sitting down, now, with booze of all kinds on the table before him. He looked up at us like a wounded giant. But none of us knew how to begin, and Callahan spoke first.

"You never did tell us your name, friend."

The alien looked startled, and he sat absolutely still, rigid as a fence post, for a long, long moment. His face twisted up awful, as though he was waging some titanic inner battle with himself, and cords of muscle stood up on his neck in what didn't seem to be the right places. Doc Webster began to talk to himself softly.

Then the alien went all blue and shivered like a steel cable under strain, and very suddenly relaxed all over with an audible gasp. He twitched his shoulders experimentally a few times, like he was making sure they were still there, and then he turned to Callahan and said, clear as a bell, "My name is Michael Finn."

It hung in the air for a very long time, while we all stood petrified, suspended.

Then Callahan's face split in a wide grin, and he bellowed, "Why of course! Why yes, yes of course, Mickey *Finn*. I didn't recognize you for a moment, Mr. Finn," as he trotted behind the bar. His big hands worked busily beneath the counter, and as he emerged with a tall glass of dark fluid the last of us got it. We made way eagerly as Callahan set the glass down before the alien, and stood back with the utmost deference and respect.

He regarded us for a moment, and to see his eyes now

was to feel warm and proud. For all the despair and guilt
and anguish and horror and most of all the hopelessness
were gone from them now, and they were just eyes. Just
like yours and mine.

Then he raised his glass and waited, and we all drank
with him. Before the last glass was empty his head hit the
table like an anvil, and we had to pick him up and carry
him to the back room where Callahan keeps a cot, and you
know, he was *heavy*.

And he snored in three stages.

2

The Time-Traveler

Of course we should have been expecting it. I guess the
people at Callahan's read newspapers just like other folks,
and there'd been a discotheque over on Jericho Turnpike
hit three days earlier. But somehow none of us was prepared for it when it came.

Well, how were we to know? It's not that Callahan's
Place is so isolated from the world that you never expect it
to be affected by the same things. God knows that most of
the troubles of the world, old and new, come through the
door of Callahan's sooner or later—but they usually have
a dollar bill in their fist, not a .45 automatic. Besides, he
was such a shrimpy little guy.

And on top of everything, it was Punday night.

Punday Night is a weekly attraction at Callahan's—if
that's the word. Folks who come into the place for the first
time on a Tuesday evening have been known to flee

screaming into the night, leaving full pitchers of beer behind in their haste to be elsewhere. There's Sunday, see, and then there's Monday, and then there's Punday. And on that day, the boys begin assembling around seven-thirty, and after a time people stop piddling around with drafts and start lining up pitchers, and Fast Eddie gets up from his beat-up upright piano and starts pulling tables together. Everyone begins ever-so-casually jockeying for position, so important on Punday night. Here and there the newer men can be heard warming up with one another, and the first groans are heard.

"Say, Fogerty. I hear tell Stacy Keach was engaged to the same girl three times. Every time the Big Day come due, she decided she couldn't stand him."

"Do tell."

"Yup. Then the late Harry Truman hisself advised her, said, 'gal, if you can't stand the Keach, get out of the hitchin.' "

And another three or four glasses hit the fireplace.

Of course the real regulars, the old-timers, simply sit and drink their beer and conserve their wit. They add little to the shattered welter of glass that grows in the fireplace—though the toasts, when they make them, can get pretty flashy.

Along about eleven Doc Webster comes waddling in from his rounds and the place hushes up. The Doc suffers his topcoat and bag to be taken from him, collects a beer-mug full of Peter Dawson's from Callahan, and takes his place at the head of the assembled tables like a liner coming into port. Then, folding his fingers over his great belly, he addresses the group.

"What is the topic?"

At this point the fate of the evening hangs in the balance. Maybe you'll get a good topic, maybe you won't —and the only way to explain what I mean is by example:

"Fast Eddie," says Callahan, "how 'bout a little inspirational music?"

"That would bring the problem into scale," says Doc Webster, and the battle is joined.

"I had already noted that," comes the hasty riposte from Shorty Steinitz, and over on his right Long-Drink McGonnigle snorts.

"You've cleffed me in twain," he accuses, and Tommy Janssen advises him to take a rest, and by the time that Callahan can point out that "This ain't a music-hall, it's a bar," they're off and running. Once a topic is established, it goes in rotation clockwise from Doc Webster, and if you can't supply a stinker when your turn comes up, you're out. By one o'clock in the morning, it's usually a tight contest between the real pros, all of them acutely aware that anyone still in the lists by closing gets his night's tab erased. It has become a point of honor to drink a good deal on Punday night to show how confident you are. When I first noticed this and asked Callahan whose idea Punday had been in the first place he told me he couldn't remember. One smart fella, that Callahan.

This one night in particular had used up an awful lot of alcohol, and one hell of a lot of spiritual fortitude. The topic was one of those naturals that can be milked for hours: "electricity." It was about one-fifteen that the trouble started.

By this point in a harrowing evening, the competition was down to the Doc, Noah Gonzalez and me. I was feeling decidedly pun-chy.

"I have a feeling this is going to be a good round Fermi," the Doc mused, and sent a few ounces of Scotch past an angelic smile.

"You've galvanized us all once again, Doc," said Noah immediately.

"Socket to me," I agreed enthusiastically.

The Doc made a face, no great feat considering what he had to work with, and glared at me. ''Wire you debasing this contest with slang?'' he intoned.

''Oh, I don't know,'' interceded Noah. ''It seems like an acceptable current usage to me.''

''You see, Doc?'' I said desperately, beginning to feel the strain now, ''Noah and I seem tube be in agreement.''

But Doc Webster wasn't looking at me. He wasn't even looking in my direction. He was staring fixedly over Noah's right shoulder. ''I regret to inform you all,'' he said with the utmost calm, ''that the gent at the bar is *not* packing a lightning rod.''

About thirty heads spun around at once, and sure enough, there was a guy in front of the bar with a .45 automatic in his hand, and Callahan was staring equably into the medicine end. He was holding out a salt-shaker in his huge horny fist.

''What's that for?'' the gunman demanded.

''Might as well salt that thing, son. You're about to eat it.''

Now your run-of-the-mill stickup artist would react to a line like that by waving the rod around a little, maybe even picking off the odd bottle behind the bar. This fellow just looked more depressed.

He didn't look like a stickup artist if it came to that; I'd have taken him for an insurance salesman down on his luck. He was short, slight and balding, and his gold-rimmed glasses pinched cruelly at his nose. His features were utterly nondescript, a Walter Mitty caricature of despair, and I couldn't help remembering that some of our more notable assassins have been Walter Mitty types.

Then I saw Fast Eddie over at the piano slide his hand down to his boot for the little blackjack he carries for emergencies, and began trying to remember if my insurance was paid up. The scrawny gunman locked eyes with Callahan, holding the cannon steady as a rock, and Callahan smiled.

"Want a drink to wash it down with?" he asked.

The guy with the gun ran out of determination all at once and lowered the piece, looking around him vaguely. Callahan pointed to the fireplace, and the guy nodded thanks. The gun described a lazy arc and landed in the pile of glass with a sound like change rattling in a pocket.

You might almost have thought the gun had shattered a window that kept out a storm, but the *whoosh*ing sound that followed was really only the noise of a couple dozen guys all exhaling at the same time. Fast Eddie's hand slid back up his leg, and Callahan said softly, "You forgot the toast, friend."

I expected that to confuse the guy, but it seemed he knew *something* about Callahan's Place after all, because he just nodded and made his toast.

"To progress."

I could see people all up and down the bar firing up their guessers, but nobody opened his trap. We waited to see if the guy felt like telling us what his beef with progress was, and when you understand that you will have gone a long way toward understanding what Callahan's Place is all about. I'm sure anywhere else folks'd figure that a man who'd just waved a gun around owed 'em an explanation, if not a few teeth. We just sat there looking noncommittal and hoping he'd let it out.

He did.

"I mean, progress is something with no pity and no purpose. It just happens. It chews up all you ever knew and spits out things you can't understand and the only value it seems to have is to make a few people a lot of money. What the hell is the sense of progress anyway?"

"Keeps the dust off ya," said Slippery Joe Maser seriously. Now Joe, as you know, has two wives, and there sure as *hell* ain't no dust on him.

"I suppose you're right," said the clerical-looking burglar, "but I'd surely appreciate a little dust just at the moment. I was hip-deep in it for years, and I didn't know how well off I was."

"Well, take this to cut it with," said Callahan, and held out a gin-and-gin. As he handed it over, his other hand came up from behind the bar with a sawed-off shotgun in it. "I'll be damned," said Callahan, noticing it for the first time, "Forgot I had that in my hand." He put it back under the bar, and the balding bandit swallowed.

"Now then, brother, pull up a chair and tell us your name, and if you've got troubles I never heard before I'll give you the case of your choice."

"Make it I. W. Harper."

"Pleased to meet you, Mr. Harp-ooooooch!" said Doc Webster, the last rising syllable occasioned by Long-drink McGonnigle's size nines having come down hard on the Doc's instep. Pretty quick on the uptake, that Long-Drink.

"My name is Hauptman," the fellow said, picking up the drink. "Thomas Hauptman. I'm a . . ." He took a long pull. "That is, I *used* to be a minister."

"And then God went and died and now what the hell do you do, is that it?" asked Long-Drink with genuine sympathy.

"Something like that," Hauptman agreed. "He died of malaria in a stinking little cell in a stinking little town in a stinking little banana republic called Pasala, and his name was Mary." Ice cubes clicked against his teeth.

"Your wife?" asked Callahan after a while.

"Yes. My wife. No one dies of malaria any more, do you know that? I mean, they licked that one years ago."

"How'd it happen?" Doc asked gently, and as Callahan refilled glasses all around, the Time-Traveler told us his story.

Mary and I (he said) had a special game we played between ourselves. Oh, all couples play the same game, I suppose, but we knew we were doing it, and we never cheated.

You see, as many of you are no doubt aware, it is often difficult for a man and a woman to agree (sustained audience demonstration, signifying hearty agreement) . . . even a minister and his wife. Almost any given course of action will have two sides: she wants to spend Sunday driving in the country, and he wants to spend it watching the football people sell razor blades.

How is the dilemma resolved? Often by histrionics, at ten paces. She will emote feverishly on the joys of a country drive, entering rapture as she portrays the heart-stopping beauty to be found along Route 25A at this time of year. He, in turn, will roll his eyes and saw his hands as he attempts to convey through the wholly inadequate vocabulary of word and gesture how crucial this particular game is to both the History of Football and the Scheme of Things.

The winner gets, in lieu of an Oscar, his or her own way.

It's a fairly reasonable system, based on the theory that the pitch of your performance is a function of how important the goal is to you. If you recognize that you're being out-acted, you realize how important this one is to your spouse, and you acquiesce.

The not-cheating comes right there—in not hamming it up just to be the winner (unless, rarely, that's the real issue), and in admitting you've been topped.

That's why when Mary brought God into the argument—a highly unfair, last-ditch gambit for a minister's wife—I gave in and agreed that we would spend my vacation visiting her sister Corinne.

I had given up a congregation over in Sayville, not very far from here. Frankly Mary and I had had all the Long Island we could take. We hadn't even any plans: we intended to take a month's vacation, our first in several years, and then decide where to settle next. I wanted to spend the month with friends in Boulder, Colorado, and Mary wanted to visit her sister in a little fly-speck banana republic called Pasala. Corinne was a nurse with the Peace Corps, and they hadn't seen each other for seven or eight years.

As I said, when a minister's wife begins to tell him about missionary zeal, it is time to capitulate. We said good-bye to my successor, Reverend Davis, promised to send a forwarding address as soon as we had one, and pushed off in the winter of 1963.

We divided the voyage between discussing the growing unpleasantness in a place called Viet Nam, and arguing over whether to ultimately settle on the West or East Coast. We both gave uncertain, shaky performances, and the issue was tabled.

Meeting Corinne for the first time I was terribly struck by a dissimilarity of the sisters. Where Mary's hair was a rich, almost chocolate brown, Corinne's was a decidedly vivid red. Where Mary's features were round, Corinne's were square, with pronounced cheekbones. Where Mary was small and soft, Corinne was long and lithe. They were both very, very beautiful, but the only characteristic they shared was a profundity of faith that had nothing to do with heredity, and which went quite as well with Corinne's fiery sense of purpose as with Mary's quiet certainty.

Pasala turned out to be a perfect comic-opera Central American country, presided over by a smalltime tyrant named De Villega. The hospital where Corinne worked was located directly across the Plaza de Palacio from the

palace which gave the square its name. De Villega had
built himself an immense mausoleum of an imitation cas-
tle from which to rule, at about the same time that the
hospital was built, with much the same sources of fund-
ing. Pasala, you see, exports maize, sugar cane, a good
deal of mahogany . . . and oil.

As Corinne led us past the palace from the harbor, I
commented on the number of heavily-armed *guardias*, in
groups of five each of which had its own *comisario*, who
stood at every point of entry to the huge stone structure
with their rifles at the ready. Corinne told us that revolution was brewing in the hills to the north, under the
leadership of a man named Miranda, who with absurd
inevitability had styled himself *El Supremo*. Mary and I
roared with laughter at this final cliché, and demanded to
be shown someone taking a siesta.

Without cracking a smile, Corinne led us around behind
the hospital, where four mule-drawn carts were filled with
khaki figures taking the siesta that never ends. "You
cannot deal with the problems of Pasala by changing the
channel, Tom," she said soberly, and my horror was
replaced by both a wave of guilt and a wistful, palpebral
vision of Boulder in the spring—which of course only
made me feel more guilty.

We dined that night in a miserable excuse for a café, but
the food was tolerable and the music quite good. Considering that the two women had not seen each other for years,
it was not surprising that the conversation flowed freely.
And it kept coming back to *El Supremo*.

"I have heard it said that his cause is just," Corinne told
us over coffee, "and I certainly can't argue otherwise. But
the hospital is filled with the by-products of his cause, and
I'm sick of revolution. It's been worse than ever since de
Villega had Miranda's brother shot."

"Good God. How did that come about?" I exclaimed.

"Pablo Miranda used to run this cafe, and he never had

a thing to do with revolution. In fact, an awful lot of militant types used to drink in a much more villainous place on the other side of town, rather than embarrass Pablo with their presence. But after *El Supremo* blew up the armory, de Villega went a little crazy. A squad of *guardias* came in the door and cut Pablo in half.

"Things have been accelerating ever since. People are afraid to travel by night, and de Villega has his thugs on double shifts. There are rumors that he's bringing in trucks, and cannon, and a lot of ammunition from the United States, for an expedition to clean out the hills, and the American Embassy is awfully tight-lipped about it."

"What kind of a ruler is de Villega?" Mary asked.

"Oh, an absolute thief. He robs the peons dry, rakes off all he can, and I'm sure the country would be better off if he'd never been born. But then, there are some conflicting reports about *El Supremo* too: some say he's a bit of a butcher himself. And of course he's a Communist, although God only knows what that means in Central America these days."

I began to reply, when we heard an ear-splitting crash from outside the cafe. Glasses danced off tables and shattered, and pandemonium broke loose. Three men scrambled to the door to see what had happened; as they reached the doorway a machinegun spoke, blowing all three back into the cafe. They lay as they fell, and Mary began to scream.

"Tom," Corinne shouted above the din of gunfire and panic-stricken people, "*we've got to get to the hospital.*"

"How do we get out?" I yelled back, rising and lifting Mary from her seat.

"This way."

Corinne led us rapidly through the jabbering crowd to a back exit, at which were gathered a good number of people too frightened to stick their heads out the door. I was inclined to agree with them, but Corinne simply walked out into the night. I glanced at Mary, she returned my gaze serenely, and we followed.

There were no sudden barks of gunfire; the revolutionaries were not really interested in anyone within the cafe, they were simply shooting anything that moved back in the plaza.

As I helped Mary through the dark streets behind Corinne I tried to figure the way back to the hospital, but I could not recall where the back door of the cafe lay in relation to the door through which we had entered. But it seemed to me that we would have to cross the plaza.

I called to Corinne and she halted. As I came up to her a volley of gunfire sounded off to our left, ending in a choking gurgle.

"Considering what you've told us about Miranda's egregious charm," I said as softly as a heaving chest would let me, "hadn't I better get you two ladies to the America Embassy? It's built like a fort." And it lay on this side of the Plaza.

"The hospital is very short-staffed, Tom," was all Corinne replied, with a total absence of facial expression or gesture. But I knew I could never equal a performance like that in a lifetime of trying. As she spun on her heel and continued walking, Mary and I exchanged a long look.

"And she's a rank amateur," I said, shaking my head sadly.

"She and I used to do summer stock together," she said, and we followed Corinne's disappearing footsteps.

Crossing the plaza turned out to be no more difficult than juggling poison darts; the few who shot at us were terrible marksmen. By the time it was necessary to cross open space, most of the fighting had centralized around the Palace itself, and both sides were in general much too busy to waste good bullets on three civilians running in the opposite direction. But as we reached the hospital, I glanced over my shoulder and saw trucks pulling around the corner of the building into the plaza, towing cannon behind them. As we raced through white corridors toward the Emergency Room I heard the first reports, then nothing.

The artillery provided by the U.S. State Department got off exactly three rounds. At that point, we later learned, a bearded man appeared on the palace balcony, overlooking the carnage in the square, and heaved something down onto the trampled sward. It was de Villega's head. Sensing the political climate with creditable speed, the uniformed cannoneers worked up a ragged cheer, and the revolution was over.

But not for us. The maimed and wounded who continued to be brought in through the night gave me my first real understanding of the term *waking nightmare*, and until you have spent a couple of hours collecting random limbs and organs for disposal I will thank you not to use the term yourself. I had rather naively assumed that the worst would be over when the battle stopped, but that turned out to be only the signal for the rape and plundering and settling of ancient grudges, which got a good deal uglier. I tried to get Mary to take a few hours of sleep, and she tried to get me to do the same, and although we both put on the performance of a lifetime neither of us would concede defeat.

It was about three the next afternoon when I heard the scream. I left one of de Villega's *rurales* to finish sewing up his own arm and sprinted down a crowded hall toward the surgery where Mary and Corinne had been for the past thirteen hours. It sounded as though the scream had come from there . . .

It had. As I burst in the door I saw Mary first, in the impersonally efficient grip of the largest man I've ever seen in my life. Then I saw Corinne, struggling with a broad-backed revolutionary who was throttling a uniformed patient on the operating table. The crossed bandoliers over his shoulders rose and fell as he strangled, as though he wanted there to be more to it than simply clenching his fingers. Corinne's flailing fists he noticed not at all.

She was undoubtedly stronger than I—I wasted no time in tugging at the madman's shoulder. I picked up the nearest heavy object, a water pitcher I believe, and bounced it off the back of his skull as hard as I could. He sighed and crumpled, and I whirled toward the giant that held my Mary.

"You should not have done that, *señor*," he said in a deep, soft voice. "The man on the bed, he once did a discourtesy to Pedro's wife. A grave discourtesy."

"Get out of this room at once," Corinne snapped in her best drill-sergeant voice, shaking with rage.

The big man shook his head sadly. "I am afraid not, *señorita*," he rumbled. Hands like shovels tightened around Mary's biceps, and she still had not uttered a sound since I burst in. "*Señor*," the giant said to me, "you must please put down that pitcher, or I will be forced to do your own wife a small discourtesy." I started. "Ah, you see? I know who you are; and I would not wish to be discourteous to the wife of a man of God."

The gorilla on the floor began to stir, and the huge man sighed. "I am afraid it is all over for you, *Padre*. Pedro, he is a most unreasonable man when he feels his honor is at stake. You hit him from behind."

Corinne snarled and leaped at him, and I followed suit. Even together we could not budge him or his iron grip, but we kept him too busy to hurt Mary, and I think we might eventually have prevailed. But suddenly something large and heavy smashed into my left kidney, and I fell to the floor gasping with pain. Through the haze I saw Pedro, his tangled hair soaked with blood on the side, step over me and reach for Mary, and my soul died in my chest.

Then my ears rang with a shot, and I twisted about on

the floor to see a tall man with a bristling mustache framed in the doorway, a smoking automatic in his hand. He wore the shapeless khakis of the mountains and there was an easy arrogance in the smile with which he regarded all of us.

Behind me there was thud as a body hit the floor. Half-blind with pain, I contrived to roll over again and saw that the pistol shot had taken off the top of Pedro's skull.

"There is that about martial law," said the man in the doorway with sardonic amusement. "It is addictive."

I finally managed to sit up, bracing myself against a large oxygen bottle. "Who are you?" I managed.

The lean, mustached man bowed low. "Permit me to introduce myself, *Padre*. I am *El Supremo e Illustrisimo Señor* Manuel Conception de Miranda, the current ruler of this republic. You in turn, are the Reverend Hauptman, and I must assume that the charming lady there—release her at once, Diego—is your wife Mary."

His excellent English bespoke an unusual degree of education, and his bearing was a studied claim to nobility. I began to believe that we three might survive the afternoon for the first time in what seemed like hours.

"How do you all seem to know who we are?" I asked. "We only arrived yesterday, and I don't think we've spoken to more than a handful of Pasalans. Yet that monster over there knew us . . . and I'm *sure* I'd remember him."

"I know all about the comings and goings of all American nationals in Pasala," he said smugly. "Your country has been a source of much inconvenience to me, and I am a thorough man, as are my lieutenants. Diego is one; Pedro there was another. I cannot abide by a lieutenant who loses his head." He holstered his gun and entered the room, and I struggled to my feet with Mary's help. We clung together, and she trembled violently.

El Supremo looked about, failed to find a place to sit.

He strode to the operating table, shoved the wounded and unconscious soldier off onto the hard floor quite casually, and sat down with his legs dangling over the edge.

Corinne went for him, but before she covered three feet the giant Diego intercepted her and lifted her clear off her feet. She struck at his face with balled fists, but he appeared not to notice. She was sobbing with rage.

"Diego," said Miranda with a grin, "since you do not seem to be content unless you have a woman in your hands, why don't you take the young lady to my apartments and keep her there until I come, eh?"

Mary and I both cried out.

"My friends," said Miranda, still grinning, "this is only justice. I had a woman, Rosa, and she was heart of my heart. She was killed last night, by an American cannon shell. Because of your country, I have no woman. It seems only fair that America give me a woman. I prefer an unmarried woman, and I do not think the sister of a minister's wife will disappoint me." He laughed, a gay laugh that froze my blood.

"There is that about martial law," I heard myself say. "It is selective."

"Explain," El Supremo barked.

"I believe the man on the floor over there was shot for attempted rape," I said quietly.

"*Padre*," said the tall revolutionary, drawing his gun again, "in the absence of a lawful constitution for Pasala I must do the best I can myself. Occasionally I may be inconsistent, as I am now in sentencing you and your wife to ten years' imprisonment for disturbing the peace.

"But you will find that there is *this* about martial law: it is effective."

The next twenty minutes were the last free minutes I would spend for ten years, and the last free minutes of Mary's life, but I don't remember one of them. *El Supremo* marched us at gunpoint across the plaza to the palace, down many flights of stairs, to the lowest of the three basement floors which made up the palace's dungeons. There he locked us personally into a nine-by-twelve stone cell, and left.

We were there for nine years, and I will not speak of those years. After Mary died, I was alone there for eleven months longer, and I will not think of those months. I will only say that in the first weeks, I thanked God for giving Miranda the spark of humanity which caused him to put both Mary and me in the same cell . . . but soon, as I began to see the subtlety and horror of his true intent, I came to curse him with a black hatred. Ten years inside a stone cube with no heat, no ventilation and a pail for a toilet can do much to a marriage, and that Mary and I survived as long as we did was, I assure you, due only to the depth and strength of her character. And even she couldn't keep me from losing my faith in God . . .

The minister was silent, staring into his glass as though he read there a strange and terrible secret which he could not quite believe. The stillness was absolute; no flames danced in the fireplace. I caught Doc Webster's eye, and he seemed to come back from somewhere else with a start.

"What happened to Corinne?" he asked hoarsely.

Hauptman put down his glass suddenly, and looked around at us incuriously. "I've been told she died that night," he said conversationally, "and I rather hope it's true. Miranda was . . . an animal."

"Couldn't the American Embassy do anything to get you out?" asked Long-Drink quickly, and I saw Callahan nod approval.

"The American Embassy," replied Hauptman bitterly, "neither had the slightest knowledge of our incarceration, nor cared to know. If anyone at all was aware of our presence in Pasala, he must have assumed we had been killed in the uprising, and he undoubtedly heaved a great sigh when he realized he had no idea who to send condolences to." His words came like machine-gun bullets now.

"We were listed in the prison records as 'Hidalgo, Tomaso and Maria, subversives,' and that was quite good enough for the State Department, if they checked at all. *El Supremo* was quite an embarrassment to the United States, and when they had him assassinated two years later, the puppet *presidentes* they installed were far too busy entertaining American oil executives to be bothered inspecting the palace dungeons. The only human we saw for nine years was a perpetually drunken jailer who brought such of our food as he didn't eat himself. I'd be there now, except that when . . . when Mary died, th-they . . ." He broke off, got a fresh grip on himself and continued, "Someone noticed her body being removed for burial, and became curious as to why Maria Hidalgo looked like an American. It was a year before I was released, owing to, let me see now, 'political complications of an extremely delicate nature in the Middle East,' I think they said . . . my god, I just realized what they meant! It sounded insane at the time, and I hadn't thought about it since." He laughed bitterly. "Well, what do you know? Anyway, for the last six months I was there I had Red Cross food and a blanket, so that was hunky-dory. Turned out there was a man from Baltimore four cells down, part of the hospital staff, and he was released too. If Mary hadn't died we'd both still be there." The minister laughed again, gulped down the rest of his gin-and-gin and made a face. "She was always getting me out of scrapes."

More gin appeared before him; he gulped it noisily.

"You know," he said with a dangerous high note in his voice, "in all the nine years the prayers never stopped rising from that filthy little cell. For the first three years, we prayed that someone would depose *El Supremo*. For approximately the next three years, Mary prayed con-

stantly that my faith in God would return. Then, for about
a year, I prayed to I-don't-know-who that Mary would
live. And after malaria took her, I spent my time praying
to anyone who would listen for a chance to kill *El Supremo*
with my own hands.

"I mean to say, isn't it ironic? All that prayer, and none
of it did the slightest good. *El Supremo* was dead all the
time, I never seemed to get that belief back, and Mary
. . ." He broke off short and began to laugh softly, a
laugh that got shriller and shriller until the glass burst in
his hand. He then just sat and looked at his bleeding palm
until Doc Webster came over and gently took it away from
him.

"Well, at least this damned thing is disinfected," the
Doc grumbled. "Don't ever pull that with an empty
glass." Someone fetched his battered black bag, and he
began applying a dressing.

Along about that point, everyone in the place got real
interested in the floor or the ceiling. It somehow didn't
seem as though there was a single intelligent thing that
could be said, and it was slowly becoming necessary that
somebody say *something*.

Callahan was right there.

"Reverend," he rumbled, hooking a thumb in his belt,
"that's a right sad story. I've heard an awful lot of blues,
and I can't say I ever heard worse. But what I would like to
have explained to me is how, if you follow me, the *hell*
does all this bring you into my joint with a heater in your
fist?" There was steel in his voice, and the minister looked
up sharply, guilt replacing the agony on his features.
Bravo, Callahan, I thought.

See, I knew what the preacher couldn't: that when
there's anger in Callahan's voice, it's just got to be theat-
rics, because when Callahan is good and truly pissed off
he don't bother to talk at all.

The little minister was a while finding words. "You

see," he said finally, as the Doc finished bandaging his hand, "it was ten years. Ten *years*. I . . . I don't know if you can understand what I mean. I know it's been two years since Mary died — it's not just that. But you see, she was all I know for such a long time, and now I don't know anything at all.

"You must understand, in all that time we never saw a newspaper or a magazine or a T.V. broadcast, never heard so much as a radio. We had utterly no communication with the outside world; we were as isolated as two human beings can be."

"Hell," said Tommy Janssen, "that sounds like what I could use to straighten out my head once and for all." I was thinking about a Theodore Sturgeon story called "And Now The News," and I kind of agreed with Tommy, which shows how well I'd read the story.

"Straighten your head out!" Hauptman exploded.

"Now, you know perfectly well what the boy means," Long-Drink interceded. "No one is saying those years weren't nightmares for you, but you know, they were nothing to write home to mother about for us. You missed a lot of turmoil, and lot of bad times and trouble, and maybe in that at least you were better off. I know most of us here have probably wished we could get away from everything for a long spell, and you did it. What's wrong with isolation?"

"Nothing, *per se*," Hauptman said quietly. "The problem is this: the world won't wait for you. You drop out for more than a short time, and brother, the world goes on without you."

"I think," said Callahan slowly, "I begin to see what you mean."

"You don't even begin," Hauptman said flatly. "You can't. You're too close to it. The whole world turns upside down in ten years, but you turn upside down with it, and so to you it's right side up. It all happens over days and weeks and months, and most people can adapt that fast. But I don't recognize the first thing about this world—I didn't live through it.

"Let me give all you good people a history lesson."

He got up, walked to the bar and put out his hand. Callahan put a glass of gin in it. He turned, faced us all, took a long swallow, and cleared his throat pedantically.

"Mary and I left for Pasala in February of 1963," he said. "I've since had occasion to supplement my own memories with references from *The New York Times*, and you may find some of them interesting.

"On the day of our departure, for instance, there had been a total of thirty-three Americans killed in Viet Nam since the start of U.S. involvement. Not that anyone was aware of it: it wasn't until a few days after we left that Senator Mansfield's study group issued a warning that the Viet Nam struggle was becoming an 'American War, that cannot be justified by present U.S. security interests in the area.' Why, the godforsaken place was costing us a whole four hundred million dollars a year!

"Of course, General O'Donnell replied the next day that all those combat pilots among the 'advisers' were there to train the Viet Namese, not to take part in the war themselves.

"Lot happened since then, hasn't it?

"How about another area, my friends? In November of 1962, Dean Munro of Harvard University warned undergraduates against use of 'the simulant L.S.D. that depresses the mind,' and censured Professors Alpert and Leary for promoting its use. Dr. Leary replied that hysteria could only hamper research, and pointed to the absence of any evidence that the drug was harmful.

"In California, meanwhile, authorities were sounding a similar warning note concerning a newly-discovered drug which was beginning to appear on the streets. It was called Methedrine.

"The New American Church was still fighting unsuccessfully for the right to continue using peyote in its religious ceremonies, a practice which predated white settlement of America. Harry Anslinger had just retired as head of the Federal Narcotics Agency, and there was some talk of controlling the sale of airplane glue to those under eighteen.

"Incidentally, while Leary and Alpert (who I understand calls himself Ram Dass lately) found little difficulty in preserving their academic autonomy, others were not so lucky. Professor Koch was fired from Illinois University for daring to suggest in print that premarital sexual relations should in some cases be condoned. By the time Mary and I got on the boat, the efforts of the American University sity Professors' Association to have him reinstated had been entirely fruitless. A month after we left, the Illinois Supreme Court declined to intervene. Whatever Masters and Johnson were doing, they weren't talking about it. The sexual revolution was still being vigorously, and apparently successfully, ignored.

"Hard to remember back ten years, isn't it? How about the space race? The latest news I've heard puts us quite a few moon landings and space probes ahead of the Russians, and most people I've spoken to seem to assume it was always that way. America has felt pretty cocky about the Big Deep for quite a while now. Did you know that by February of 1963, the Russian Vostok series had racked up 130 orbits, a total of 192 hours in space, while the U.S. had a total of 12 orbits and 20 hours? A couple of years earlier, President Kennedy—remember him?—had publicly committed us to putting a man on the moon in the next decade, and he was widely pronounced deranged. Eight years later, Armstrong took the first lunar walk, and the nation yawned. *Oh, you people are so damned blasé about it all!*

"I could go on for hours. When I dropped out, assassi-
nation had not yet become commonplace; J.F.K. had not
yet been canonized, and R.F.K. was just arguing his first
case in any court, as Attorney General of the United
States. Cinerama was just getting started, hailed as the
wave of the future, and the New York World's Fair had
not yet opened. Two months after we left, Cleopatra
premiered, and Twentieth Century-Fox stock dropped two
dollars a share—"

Hauptman broke off, began to laugh hysterically. Callahan reached across the bar and gripped his shoulder with
a hand like a steak, but the minister shook his head.

"I'm all right," he managed, choking with laughter.
"It's just that I haven't told you the funniest joke of all.
Nearly killed me at the time, and I didn't dare break up.

"You see, when I was finally released, they brought me
directly to Washington, where some very cheerless men
wanted to ask me a number of questions and help me
memorize what had officially happened. But first they
decided to compensate me for my troubles with the thrill
of a lifetime. I was conveyed before the President of the
United States for a hearty handclasp, and I thought I was
going to faint from holding in the laughter.

"I hadn't thought to ask who the President was, you
see. It didn't seem especially important, after all I'd been
through, and I didn't expect I'd recognize the name. But
when Richard Nixon held out his hand, I thought I'd die.

"—You see, three months before I left, Nixon lost the
race for governor of California, and assured the press with
tears in his eyes that they wouldn't have Dick Nixon to
kick around any more . . ."

This time the whole place broke up, and Doc Webster
almost lost his tonsils trying to whoop and swallow at the
same time. Fast Eddie tried to swing into "Don't Make
Promises You Can't Keep," but he was laughing so hard

he couldn't find the keys, and a barrage of glasses hit the fireplace from all around the room.

Which was fine for catharsis. But as the laughter trailed off we realized that this catharsis was not enough for Tom Hauptman. As his impassioned words sank in it began to dawn on all of us that we had adapted to an awful lot in ten years, and in some crazy way this confrontation with a man who was forced to try and swallow a whole new world in one gulp seemed to drive home to all of us just how imperfectly we *had* adapted, ourselves.

"You know," Long-Drink drawled in the sudden silence, "the little man has a point. Been a lot goin' on lately."

"It occurs to me," Tommy Janssen said softly, "that ten years ago I'd never heard the word *heroin*," and he gulped at his beer.

"Ten years ago," Doc Webster mused, "I thought that heart transplants were the province of science-fiction writers."

"Ten years ago," Slippery Joe breathed wistfully, "I was single."

I was thinking that ten years ago, I wore a crewcut and listened to Jerry Lee Lewis and Fats Domino. "Christ," I said, as the impossible burst over me. "Nobody'd ever heard of the *Beatles* in 1963!" The whole electric sound, the respectability of rock and its permeation of all other forms of pop music, had taken place while Hauptman was rotting in a cell, listening to his fingernails growing. What must the music of today sound like to him? Jim McGuinn of the Byrds had pointed out in the late Sixties that the Beatles had signaled a change in the very sound of music. He compared pre-Beatles music to the bass roar of a propellor plane, and the ensuing post-Beatles rock to the metallic whine of a jet engine. From what I hear on the radio, it seems that we're already up to the transonic shrieking of a rocket exhaust, and Hauptman was getting it all at once. From Paul Anka to Alice Cooper in one jump! Why, the sartorial and tonsorial changes alone were enough to boggle the mind.

We all stared at him, thinking we understood. But he looked around at us and shook his head, and took another drink.

"No," he said. "You still don't understand. What you are all just beginning to see is what I would, if I were a science-fiction writer, call the Time Traveler's Dilemma: *future shock*, I believe they're calling it now. But my problem is the Time Traveler's Second Dilemma: *transplant shock*.

"You see, you're all time-travelers, too, traveling through time at a rate of one second per second. In the past few minutes, you've all been made acutely aware of just how much time you've passed through in the last ten years, and it's made you think.

"But I've traveled ten years all at once, and I don't have your advantages. Strange as this particular time is to you, you have roots woven into its fabric, you have a place in it however tenuous, and most important of all, you have a *purpose*.

"Don't you understand? I was a *minister*.

"I was charged with responsibility for the spiritual development of other human beings. I was trained to help them live moral lives, to make right choices in difficult decisions, and to comfort them when they needed comfort. And now I don't even begin to grasp their *problems*, let alone the new tools that people like me have been jury-rigging over the past ten years to help them. Why, I went to a fellow cleric for advice, and he offered me a marijuana cigarette! I called an old acquaintance of mine, a Catholic priest, and his wife answered the phone; I told her I had a wrong number and hung up. This whole

Watergate Affair is no revelation to anyone who was in Pasala in 1963; it's been a long time since I believed Uncle Sam was a virgin. But I used to be in the minority.

"Gentlemen, how can I function as a minister when I don't even begin to comprehend *one single one* of the moral issues of the day? When I can't, because I haven't lived through the events that gave them birth?"

He finished off his gin, left the glass on the table and began tracing designs in the moisture it had left there.

"I've looked for other work. I've looked for other work for nearly six months now. Are any of you here out of work?"

Which was a shame, him saying that, because it caused me to pitch a perfectly good glass of Bushmill's into the fireplace.

Hauptman nodded, and turned to the red-haired mountain behind the bar.

"And that, Mr. Callahan," he said quietly, "is the long and short of why you find me in your establishment with a pistol I bought in an alleyway from a young man with more hair than Mary used to have. I simply didn't know what else to do."

He looked around at all of us.

"And now that didn't work either. So there's only one thing left I can do." He heaved a great sigh, and his shoulders twitched. "I wonder if I'll get to see Mary again?"

Now, we're a reasonably bright bunch at Callahan's (with some notable exceptions), and nobody in the room figured that the one thing Hauptman had left to do was start up a chain-letter. But at the same time, we're a humane bunch, with a fanatical concern for individual liberty, and so we couldn't do any of the conventional things, like try to talk him out of it, or call the police, or have him fitted for the jacket that's all sleeves. Truth to tell, maybe one or two of us agreed with him that he had no alternative. We were pretty shaken by his story, is all I can say in our defense.

Because we just sat there, and stared at him, and felt helpless, and the silence became a tangible thing that throbbed in your temples and made your eyes sting.

And then Callahan cleared his throat.

"To be or not to be," he declaimed in a voice like a foghorn. "Is that the question?"

Like I said, we're a bright bunch, but it took us a second. By the time I got it, Callahan had already lumbered out from behind the bar, swept a pitcher and three glasses to the floor, and wrapped the tablecloth around him like a toga. Doc Webster was grinning openly.

"Listen, ya goddam fathead," Callahan declaimed in the hokey, stentorian tones of a Shakespearean ham, " 'tis damn well *nobler* to suffer the slings and arrows of outrageous fortune, than to take arms against a sea of troubles, and by opposing, let 'em lick ya. Nay, fuck that . . ." His eyes rolled, his huge hands sawed the air as he postured and orated.

Hauptman stared blankly, his mouth open.

Doc Webster heaved himself up onto a chair, *harummph*ed noisily and struck a pose.

"Do not go gentle into that good night," he began passionately.

Suddenly Callahan's Place became a madhouse, something like a theater might be if actors "tuned-up" as cacaphonously as do orchestras. Everyone suddenly became the Ghost of Barrymore, or thought he had, and the air filled with praises of life and courage delivered in the most impassioned histrionic manner. I unpacked my old guitar and joined Fast Eddie in a rousing chorus of "Pack Up Your Sorrows," and I guess among us all we made a hell of a racket.

"All right, all right," Callahan bellowed after a few

minutes of pandemonium. "I reckon that ought to do, gents. *I* think we took the Oscar."

He turned to Hauptman, and tossed the tablecloth on the floor.

"Well, Reverend," he growled. "Can you top that performance?"

The little minister looked at him for a long spell, and then he began to laugh and laugh. It was a different kind of laugh than we'd heard from him before: it had no ragged edges and no despair in it. It was a full, deep belly-laugh, and instead of grating on our nerves like a knife on piano wire it made us feel warm and proud and relieved. Kind of a tribute to our act.

"Gentlemen," he said finally, clapping his hands feebly, still chuckling, "I concede. I've been out-acted fair and square; I wouldn't try to compete with a performance like that."

Then all at once he sobered, and looked at all of us. "I . . . I didn't know people like you existed in this world. I . . . I think that I can make it now. I'll find some kind of work. It's just that . . . well . . . *if somebody else knows how tough it is, then it's all right.*" The corners of his mouth, lifting in a happy smile, met a flood of tears on their way down. "Thank you, my friends. Thank you."

"Any time," said Callahan, and meant it.

And the door banged inevitably open, and we spun around to see a young black kid, chest heaving, framed in the doorway with a .38 Police Positive in his hand.

"Now everybody be quiet, an' nobody gonna get hurt," he said shrilly, and stepped inside.

Callahan seemed to swell around the shoulders, but he didn't move. Everybody was frozen, thinking for the second time that night that *we should have been expecting it,* and of all of us only Hauptman refused to be numbed by shock any more, only Hauptman kept his head, and only Hauptman remembered.

It all happened very quickly then, as it had to happen. Callahan's shotgun was behind the bar, out of reach, and Fast Eddie had been caught with both hands in sight. The minister caught Doc Webster's eye, and they exchanged a meaningful glance across the room that I didn't understand.

And then the Doc cleared his throat. "Excuse me, young man," he began, and the black kid turned to tell him to shut up, and behind him Hauptman sprang from his chair headlong across the room and headfirst toward the fireplace.

He landed on his stomach, and his hands plowed straight into the welter of broken glass. As he wrenched over on his back, his right hand came around with that big .45 in it, and the kid was still turning to see what that noise behind him was.

They froze that way for a long moment, Hauptman sprawled in the fireplace, the kid by the bar, and two gun-muzzles stared unblinking across the room at each other. Then Callahan spoke.

"You'll hurt him with a .38 son, but he'll kill you with a .45."

The kid froze, his eyes darting around the room, then flung his gun from him and bolted for the door with a noise like a cross between a sneeze and a sob. Nobody got in his way.

And then Callahan spoke up again. "You see, Tom," he said conversationally, "moral issues never change. Only social ones."

One thing I'll say for the boys at Callahan's: they can keep a straight face. Nobody cracked a smile as Callahan fed the cops a perfectly hilarious yarn about how the minister had disarmed a thief with a revolver he had only that afternoon taken from a troubled young parishioner. Some of us had even argued against involving the police at all, on general principles—I was one of them—but Callahan insisted that he didn't want any guns in his joint, and nobody else really wanted them either.

But when I was proudest of the boys was when the police asked for a description of the thief. None of us had given any thought to that, but Doc Webster was right in there, his dragon-in-the-shower voice drowning out all others.

"Description?" he boomed. "Hell, nobody was ever easier to describe. The guy was six-four with a hook-nose, blonde hair, blue eyes, a scar from his right ear to his chin and he had one leg."

And not one of us so much as blinked as the cop dutifully wrote that down.

Perhaps that kid would have another chance.

Tom Hauptman, however, didn't come off so well in the aplomb department. As one of the cops was phoning in, Long-Drink called out, "Hey Tom. One thing I don't understand. That cannon you had was in the fireplace for a good hour or so, and that hearth is plenty warm even when the fire's been out a while. How the hell come none of the cartridges went off?"

The minister looked puzzled. "Why, I have no idea. Do you suppose that . . .?"

But the second cop was making strangling sounds and waving the .45. At last he found his voice. "You mean you *didn't know?*"

We looked at him.

He tossed the gun to Callahan, who one-handed it easily, then suddenly looked startled. He hefted the gun, and his jaw dropped.

"There's no clip in this gun," he said faintly. "The damned thing's unloaded."

And Tom Hauptman fainted dead away.

By the time we recovered from that one, Callahan had decided that Doc and Noah and I were Punday Night Champions, and we were helping ourselves to just one more free drink with Tom Hauptman when Doc came up with an idea.

"Say, Mike," he called out. "Don't you think a bunch of savvy galoots like us could find Tom here some kind of job?"

"Well, I'll tell you, Doc," said Callahan, scratching his neck, "I've been givin' that some thought." He lit a cigar and regarded the minister with a professional eye. "Tom, do you know anything about tending bar?"

"Huh? Why, yes I do. I tended bar for a couple of summers before I entered the ministry."

"Well," Callahan drawled, "I ain't getting any younger. This all day and all night stuff is okay for someone your age, but I'm pushing fifty. Why I hit a man last week, and he got up on me. I've been meaning to get myself a little part-time help, sorta distribute the load a little. And I'd be right honored to have a man of God serve my booze."

A murmur of shock ran through the bar, and expression of awe at the honor being accorded to Tom Hauptman. He looked around, having the sense to see that it was up to us as much as it was to Callahan.

"Why the hell not?" roared Long-Drink and the Doc together, and the minister began to cry.

"Mr. Callahan," he said, "I'd be proud to help you run this bar."

About that point a rousing cheer went up, and about two dozen glasses met above the newly-relit blaze in the fireplace. Toasts got proposed all at once, and a firecracker went off somewhere in the back of the room. The minister was lifted up onto a couple or three shoulders, and the most godawful alleycat off-key chorus you ever heard assured him that he was indeed a Jolly Good Fellow.

"This calls for another drink," Callahan decreed. "What'll it be, Tom?"

"Well," the minister said diffidently, "I've had an awful lot of gin, and I really haven't gotten back into training yet. I think I'd better just have a Horse's Ass."

"Reverend," said Callahan, vastly chagrined, "whatever it is, you're gonna get it on the house. 'Cause I never heard of it."

All around the room conversations chopped off in midsentence as the news was assimilated. The last time in my memory when Callahan got taken for a drink was in 1968, when some joker in a pork-pie hat asked for a Mother Superior. Turned out to be a martini with a prune in it, and Callahan by God went out and bought a prune.

Hauptman blinked at the commotion he was causing, and finally managed, "Well, it, uh, won't set you back very much. It's just a ginger ale with a cherry in it." He paused, apparently embarrassed, and continued just a shade too diffidently, "You see, they call it that be—"

"—CAUSE ANYONE WHO'D ORDER ONE IS A HORSE'S ASS!" chorused a dozen voices with him, and a shower of peanuts hit him from all over the room. Tommy Janssen heaved a half-full pitcher at the fireplace, and Fast Eddie snatched it out of the air with his right hand as his left picked up "You Said It, Not Me" in F sharp.

Hauptman accepted his drink from Callahan, and he had it to his lips before he noticed the remarkably authentic-looking plastic fly which Callahan had thoughtfully added to the prescription. The explosion was impressive, and I swear ginger ale came out his ears.

"Seemed like a likely place to find a fly," said Callahan loudly, and somehow Fast Eddie managed to heave the pitcher at him without interrupting the song. Callahan fielded it deftly and took a long drink.

"That's what I like to see," he boomed, replacing his cigar in his teeth. "A place that's *merry*."

3

The Centipede's Dilemma

What happened to Fogerty was a classic example of the centipede's dilemma. Served him right, of course, and I suppose it was bound to happen sooner or later. But things could have gone much worse with him if he hadn't been wearing that silly hat.

It was this way:

Fogerty came shuffling in to Callahan's Place for the first time on the night of the Third Annual Darts Championship of the Universe, an event by which we place much store at Callahan's, and I noticed him the moment he walked in. No great feat; he was a sight to see. He looked like a barrel with legs, and I mean a big barrel. On its side. On top of this abundance sat a head like a hastily peeled potato, and on top of the head sat—or rather sprawled—the most ridiculous hat I'd ever seen. It could have passed for a dead zeppelin, floppy and disheveled, a villainous yellow in color. From the moment I saw it I expected it ot slide down his face like a disreputable avalanche, but some mysterious force held it at eyebrow level. I couldn't estimate his age.

Callahan served him without blinking an eye—I sometimes suspect that if a pink gorilla walked into Callahan's, on fire, and ordered a shot, Callahan would ask if it wanted a chaser. The guy inhaled three fingers of gin in as many seconds, had Callahan build him another, and strolled on over to the crowd by the dart board, where Long-Drink McGonnigle and Doc Webster were locked in mortal combat. I followed along, sensing something zany in the wind.

Some of us at Callahan's are pretty good with a dart, and consequently the throwing distance is thirty feet, a span which favors brute strength but requires accuracy along with it. The board is a three foot circle with a head-shot of a certain politician (supply your own) on its face, concentric circles of fifty, forty, twenty, ten and one point each superimposed over his notorious features. When I got to where I could see the board Doc Webster had just planted a dandy high on the right cheek for fourty, and Long-Drink was straining to look unconcerned.

"What's the stakes?" the guy with the hat asked me. His voice sounded like a '54 Chevy with bad valves.

"Quarts of Scotch," I told him. "The challenger stakes a bottle against the previous winner's total. Last year the Doc there went home with six cases of Peter Dawson's." He grunted, watched the Doc notch an ex-presidential ear (you supplied the same politician, didn't you?), then asked how he could sign up. I directed him to Fast Eddie, who was taking a night off from the piano to referee, and kept half an eye on him while I watched the match. He took no part in the conversational hilarity around him, but watched the combat with a vacuous stare, rather like a man about to fall asleep before the T.V. It was reasonably apparent that wit was not his long suit. Doc Webster won the match handily, and the stein that Long-Drink disconsolately pegged into the big fireplace joined a mound of broken glass that was mute testimony to the Doc's prowess. One of my glasses was in that pile.

About a pound of glass later, Fast Eddie called out, "Dink Fogerty," and the guy with the hat stood up. The Doc beamed at him like a bear being sociable to a hive, and offered him the darts.

They made a quite a pair. If Fogerty was a barrel, the Doc is what they shipped the barrel in, and it probably rattled a lot. Fogerty took the darts, rammed them together point-first into a nearby table-top, and stood back smiling. The Doc blinked, then smiled back and toed the mark. Plucking a dart from the table-top with an effort, he grinned over his shoulder at Fogerty and let fly.

The dart missed the board entirely.

A gasp went up from the crowd, and the Doc frowned. Fogerty's expression was unreadable. The champ plucked another dart, wound up and threw again.

The dart landed in the fireplace fifteen feet to the left with a noise like change rattling in a pocket.

"It curved," the Doc yelped, and some of the crowd guffawed. But from where I stood I could see that there were four men between Doc Webster and the fireplace, and I could also see the beginnings of an unpleasant smile on Fogerty's thick features.

None of the Doc's remaining shots came close to the target, and he left the firing line like a disconsolate blimp, shaking his head and looking at his hand. Fogerty took his place and, without removing that absurd hat, selected a dart.

Watching his throw I thought for a second the match might turn out a draw. His wind-up was pitiful, his stance ungainly, and he held the dart too near the feathers, his other arm stiff at his side. He threw like a girl, and his follow-through was nonexistent.

The dart landed right between the eyes with a meaty *thunk*.

"Winner and new champeen, Dink Fogerty," Fast Eddie hollered over the roar of the crowd, and Fogerty took a long, triumphant drink from the glass he'd set down on a nearby table. Fat Eddie informed him that he'd just won thirty-five bottles of Scotch, and the new champ smiled, turned to face us.

"Any takers?" he rasped. The '54 Chevy had gotten a valve job.

"Sure," said Noah Gonzalez, next on the list. "Be damned if you'll take us for three dozen bottles with one throw." Fogerty nodded agreeably, retrieved his dart from the target and toed the mark again. And with the same awkward, off-balance throw as before, he proceeded to place all six darts in the fifty-circle.

By the last one the silence in the room was complete, and Noah's strangled "I concede," was plainly audible. Fogerty just looked smug and took another big gulp of his drink, set it down on the same table.

"Ten dollars says you can't do that again," the Doc exploded, and Fogerty smiled. Fast Eddie went to fetch him the darts, but as he reached the target . . .

"*Hold it!*" Callahan bellowed, and the room froze. Fogerty turned slowly and stared at the big redheaded barkeep, an innocent look on his pudding face. Callahan glared at him, brows like thunderclouds.

"Whassamatter, chief?" Fogerty asked.

"Damned if I know," Callahan rumbled, "but I've seen you take at least a dozen long swallows from that drink you got, and it's *still full*."

Every eye in the place went to Fogerty's glass, and sure enough. Not only was it full, all the glasses near it were emptier than their owners remembered leaving them, and an angry buzzing began.

"Wait a minute," Fogerty protested. "My hands've been in plain sight every minute—all of you saw me. You can't pin nothin' on me."

"I guess you didn't use your hands, then," Callahan

said darkly, and a great light seemed to dawn on Doc Webster's face.

"By God," he roared, "a telekinetic! Why you low-down, no-good . . ."

Fogerty made a break for the door, but Fast Eddie demonstrated the veracity of his name with a snappy flying tackle that cut Fogerty down before he covered five yards. He landed with a crash before Long-Drink McGonnigle, who promptly sat on him. "Tele-what?" inquired Long-Drink conversationally.

"Telekinesis," the Doc explained. "Mind over matter. I knew a telekinetic in the Army who could roll sevens as long as you cared to watch. It's a rare talent, but it exists. And this bird's got it. Haven't you, Fogerty?"

Fogerty blustered for awhile, but finally he broke down and admitted it. A lot of jaws dropped, some bouncing off the floor, and Long-Drink let the guy with the hat back up, backing away from him. The hat still clung gaudily to his skull like a homosexual barnacle.

"You mean you directed dem darts wit' yer mind?" Fast Eddie expostulated.

"Nah. Not ezzackly. I . . . I make the dart-board *want darts*."

"Huh?"

"I can't make the darts move. What I do, I project a . . . a state of wanting darts onto the center of the target, like some kinda magnet, an' the target attracts 'em for me. I only learned how ta do it about a year ago. The hard part is to hang on to all but one dart."

"Thought so," growled Callahan from behind the bar. "You make your glass want gin, too—don't ya?"

Fogerty nodded. "I make a pretty good buck as a fisherman—my nets want fish."

It seemed to me that, given his talent, Fogerty was making pretty unimaginative use of it. Imagine a cancer wanting X-rays. Then again, imagine a pocket that wants diamonds. I decided it was just as well that his ambitions were modest.

"Wait a minute," said the Doc, puzzled. "This 'state of wanting darts' you project. What's it like?"

And Fogerty, an unimaginative man, pondered that question for the first time in his life, and the inevitable happened.

There's an old story about the centipede who was asked how he could coordinate so many legs at once, and, considering the mechanics of something that had always been automatic, became so confused that he never managed to walk again. In just this manner, Fogerty focused his attention on the gift that had always been second nature to him, created that zone of yearning for the first time in his head where he could observe it, and . . .

The whole half-dozen darts ripped free of the target, crossed the room like so many Sidewinder missiles, and smashed into Fogerty's forehead.

If he hadn't been wearing that dumb hat, they might have pulped his skull. Instead they drove him backward, depositing him on his ample fundament, where he blinked up at us blinking down at him. There was a stunned silence (literally so on his part) and then a great wave of laughter that grew and swelled and rang, blowing the cobwebs from the rafters. We laughed till we cried, till our lungs ached and our stomachs hurt, and Fogerty sat under the avalanche of mirth and turned red and finally began to giggle himself.

And like the centipede, like the rajah whose flying carpet would only function if he did *not* think of the word "elephant," Fogerty from that day forth never managed to bring himself to use his bizarre talent again.

Imagine getting a netfull of mackerel in the eye!

4

Two Heads Are Better Than One

As usual, it was a pretty merry night at Callahan's when the trouble started.

I don't want to give the impression that every time us Callahan's regulars (Callahanians?) get to feeling good, there's drama around the corner. The reason it seems that way is probably that, barring disaster, merriment is the general rule at Callahan's Place. Most of us have little better to do than get happy in another's company, and we're not an unimaginative bunch, so we keep ourselves pretty well amused.

Being a Wednesday, it was Tall Tales Night (as opposed to Monday, the Fireside Fill-More singalong night, or Tuesday, which we call Punday). Along about eight-thirty, when most of the boys had arrived, and the level of broken glass in the fireplace was still rather low, Callahan dried his big meaty hands on his apron and cleared his throat with a sound like a bulldozer in pain.

All right gents," he boomed, and conversations were tabled for the night. "We need a subject. Any suggestions?"

Nobody spoke up. See, the teller of the tallest tale on a Wednesday night gets his drinking money refunded, and most folks like to lie low until they've had a chance to examine the competition and come up with a topper. Not that the first tale told never wins, but it has to be pretty memorable.

"All right," Callahan said when no one took the lead. "People, places or things?"

"We did t'ings last week," Fast Eddie pointed out from his seat at the upright. True enough. I'd had everybody beat with a yarn about a beer-nut tree that used to grow in my backyard until I watered it, when Doc Webster wiped me out with the saga of a '38 Buick of his that understood spoken English, which would have been just fine except that it took on a rude highway cop one day and chased him across six lanes of traffic. Doc claimed to have buried it in his backyard after it expired from remorse.

"Ain't nothing says we have to be consistent," Callahan replied. "We can do things again."

"Naw," Doc Webster called out. "Let's do people."

"All right, Doc. What kind? You sound like you got something in mind."

"Wal . . ." drawled the Doc, and people checked to see that their drinks were fresh. Those who needed a refill put a dollar bill on the bar and were refueled by Callahan, who did not need to ask what they wanted.

". . . I was just thinking," the Doc continued, his own drink as magically full as always, "of my Cousin Hobart, the celebrated Man With The Foot-Long Nose." ("Oh, relatives tonight," someone muttered.) "Hobart's mother died in childbirth, naturally, and his father succumbed to acute embarrassment shortly thereafter. As a child Hobart was a born showman, keeping the orphanage in stitches with incredibly accurate woodpecker imitations, and upon attaining the age of seven he ran away, to form the nucleus of a traveling road company which played *Pinocchio* in every theater in the country, and some in the city too. This kept him in Kleenex until he outgrew the role, and *Cyrano de Bergerac* was not popular at the time, so he struck off on his own and in short order became something of an old stand-by on the vaudeville circuits, where his ability to identify the perfume of ladies in the last row and his prowess on the nose-flutes (as many as five at one time) were a never-failing draw. He might have lived on in this way for a good many years, for he was a fanatically hygienic man, and although there were dark rumors about his sex life he was invariably discreet. The young ladies he visited were for some reason equally reticent, even with their best girl friends—let alone their husbands.

"No, it was not a cuckold's knuckles (say that three times fast with ice-cubes in your mouth and you can have this drink) that finally put an end to Cousin Hobart's career, though it might have been. It was by his own hand that, if I may put it this way, The Nose was blown. One night he retired early with only a slight head-cold for company, a yard-long handkerchief knotted to the bed-stead (Hobart went through a lot of laundresses before he found one with a strong stomach). Thrashing in his sleep, he rolled over and contrived to wedge the end of his nose in his right ear. Sensing some obstruction, the mighty proboscis sneezed—and damned near blew his brains out.

"When his head had stopped ringing, a wide-awake Hobart settled down to some cold hard thinking. The incident could happen again at any time—the miracle was that so likely a phenomenon had taken so long to first occur—and next time the airseal might be better. Only by chance had Hobart survived at all. He reached his decision reluctantly, but he was a brave man: he followed through. He had his nose entirely amputated the next day, repudiating all nose-hood and installing a suction cup in the middle of his glasses. Within a week he had landed a job with some moonshiners, and he works their still there still."

The Doc took a long gulp of Peter Dawson's and looked around expectantly, blinking.

There was a silence, not much thicker than an elephant's behind.

"A moonshiner with *no nose*?" snorted Long-Drink, who keeps a still in his garage for Sundays when Callahan's is closed. "That's ridiculous. How did he smell?"

"Terrible," the Doc replied placidly. "Those moonshiners are *filthy*."

A general groan began, but Callahan held up a hand. "What's the moral, Doc?"

The Doc blinked again. "No nose is good nose."

The sky rained peanuts, and very few missed the Doc, his more-than-ample upholstery making him an excellent target. Callahan, maddened beyond endurance, seized up a seltzer bottle and was restrained with some difficulty. Me, I was worried. This would be hard to beat. I decided against another Bushmill's.

As I recall, the next one up was Shorty Steinitz, with the story of his uncle Mort D. Arthur the magician, who walked down the street one day and turned into a drugstore. But three of us shouted the punchline before he got to it and he pitched his glass into the fire in disgust, toasting "To weisenheimers" first and putting his shoulder behind it. Then Tommy Janssen did a creditable job, W. C. Fields-style and better done than Fields usually is, about a Cousin Alex Ameche who used to hang from a hook on his kitchen wall and claim to be a telephone.

"Obviously a masochist," Tommy intoned nasally. "The amount of abuse that man absorbed was simply incredible. Folks'd try to humor him, put a dime in his left ear, pick up his right hand from where it hung in his other ear, dial his nose in a circle and listen to his hand. But when nothing transpired, they would inevitably beat him about the head and shoulders until the dime came out of his mouth, dislocate his arm at the shoulder and leave the premises in a great rage, cursing prodigiously." This was pretty good stuff, but Tommy's moral, "A chameleon would do well to imitate objects of a species with which

Man is not at war,'' had no pun in it, and it seemed the Doc still (the Doc's still) had the edge. Noah Gonzalez's effort, a one-joke story about an overaggressive uncle who customarily turned on the T.V. with such ferocity that one day the T.V. turned on him, was an obvious loser. For some crazy reason as each tale-teller realized he'd blown it and would thus be paying his night's tab, he invariably pitched his glass into the fireplace—which costs you your fifty cents change. Callahan had raked in a fortune in dollar bills by the time I was ready to make my move, and I decided for the hundredth time that Callahan is no fool, even if he does have to sweep out that fireplace every morning.

"All right," I said at last, "it's time to tell you good people about my Grandfather Stonebender." I decided my country drawl would serve best.

"You stole that from Heinlein," shouted Noah, the only other SF freak in the room. "One of the characters in 'Lost Legacy'' had a Grandfather Stonebender who could do anything better than anyone. No fair lifting stories.''

"Heinlein must of heard about the real Grandfather Stonebender from my grandmother,'' I said with dignity, "and at that he toned him down for a cynical public. I'm talking about the *real* Stonebender—the man who built the pyramids, freed the slaves, invented the prophylactic, cured yaws—that Stonebender.''

"What's yaws?" Callahan asked injudiciously.

"Why thanks, Mike. I'll have a beer.''

A cheer went up, and Callahan made a ferocious face at me as he drew a draft Bud. "Not that Grandfather Stonebender's legendary success was surprisin',' ' I continued smoothly, "as he was born with three heads. His mother was frightened by a pawn shop while she was carrying him. Doctor was so startled he swore off the sauce, and the child raised up such a fuss cryin' three ways at once that they sent him home early, where he caused his mother some unforseen and unprecedented difficulties with nursing.

"Fortunately, he matured quickly and found early employ as the 'before,' 'during' and 'after' for hair-tonic commercials. Which anyway kept him in hair-tonic. 'Fore too long, though, his combined I.Q. had brought him th prominence he deserved in several unrelated fields, and he passed his weekends doing a trio at the local ginmill for relaxation. *His* sex-life was something incredible, his prenatal trauma also having left him with three . . . but that's neither here nor anywheres I should be talkin' about. Point is, he wasn't no loser like Doc's cousin Hobart, reduced to geekin' in sideshows for a livin'. Grandfather Stonebender lived entirely off his wits—had to, to keep himself in neckties.

"But the same strange fate that provided him with three times the brains and earning power of a normal man carried with it the seeds of his destruction. He fell prey to the Committee Syndrome.

"One day he was debating Free Silver with himself. It was a burnin' issue at the time, and sad to say, he lost. This made him so mad he punched hisself right in the mouth, and broke several teeth and a knuckle. Bein' a gentleman, he had no alternative: he challenged hisself to a duel. Next mornin', acting as second for both sides so as to keep it in the family, he shot hisself in the right eye from point-blank range and died. Papers were full of it at the time. 'Course, if you read the only daily around you know the papers are still full of it, but anyhow that's how my Grandfather Stonebender passed on, from the past on.''

Doc Webster's mouth hung open in astonishment, but Callahan again called for the moral before the general outrage could begin.

"Just goes to show," I explained, "that three heads are bitter, then none." I closed my eyes and waited for the holocaust, smugly sure that I wouldn't have to rely on cheap gags to get free beer any more tonight.

But the silence was broken not by groans, but by a single groan, and the pain in that groan was not put-on at all. It came from the open doorway across the room, and as we all spun around we beheld a sandy-haired young man, shockingly disheveled, leaning against the doorframe and sobbing. As we watched, frozen, he slid from its support and fell full-length into Callahan's, landing on his face with a crash.

Somehow I knew intuitively that I was not a winner tonight after all.

For all his bulk, Doc Webster was the first to reach the newcomer. He rolled him over and began doing doctor-things almost before the rest of us had started to move, and swung his great black bag in a lethal circle when we crowded too close. Nobody ignores pain in Callahan's Place, but I guess sometimes we're a hair too eager to help.

The kid wasn't much older than Tommy Janssen, maybe twenty-five or so, but you had to look past the haunted lines of his face to see it. At first glance he might have been thirty or better, and the expression he'd worn before he passed out would have looked more at home on a man eighty years old and tired of living. His eyes were set in close against a hooking nose, and his cheeks were broad enough to make his mouth seem a shade too small. His lips were the kind of full that isn't especially sensual, and his frame had just a bit more meat than it needed. His clothes seemed to have been pulled on in the dark in a hell of a hurry, fly unzipped, shirt only partially tucked in and buttons mismatched with holes. Furthermore he was dressed for June—and it was a particularly rainy March out. He was soaked clear through, hair that looked usually brushed back lying limply across half his face.

It looked like he'd gotten to Callahan's just about in time.

His upper cheeks and temples were livid with purple bruises, and his knuckles were swollen. Doc Webster searched his hair and found more contusions beneath. "Looks like somebody gave this poor bastard an awful beating," the Doc announced.

The kid's eyes opened. "That was me," he said feebly, swallowing something foul.

Someone fed the Doc a glass of straight rye, and he tipped a little of it into the kid's mouth. It seemed to help. Color came back to his pasty face, and he tried to get up. The Doc told him to lie quiet, but the kid shook him off and made it as far as the first table, where he fell into a chair and looked around groggily. He didn't seem to notice us, but whatever he was expecting to see scared him silly.

It wasn't there; he relaxed some. Callahan was already piling corned beef sandwiches in front of him, and the table happened to have a pitcher of somebody's beer already on it. Throwing us all a grateful glance, *see*ing us this time, he fell on the food like the wolves upon the centerfold, and got outside of three sandwiches in short order, washing them down with great draughts of beer.

When he was done he looked Callahan squarely in the eye. "I don't have any money to pay you," he said.

"I didn't figure you did," Callahan agreed. "Go on, eat up. They were getting stale—these bums here don't eat, far as I can tell. You can owe me." He produced more food.

"Thanks. I'm O.K. now. I think. For a while."

The Doc wanted to get something straight. "You put them bruises on your own head, young feller?"

"Jim MacDonald, Doctor. Yes, I put most of those there.

"I'll bet it felt good when you stopped," Long-Drink

said, and immediately regretted it. I wouldn't want Doc Webster's mass balanced on my toe either.

"If it did, I might stop more often," MacDonald said with a ghost of a grin, wincing at the sudden pain in his temples. "Lately it's the most fun I have."

"Want to talk about it?" Callahan suggested delicately.

"Sure, why not? You'll never believe me anyhow. No one would." MacDonald's grin was gone now.

Callahan drew himself up and registered wounded dignity. "Son, this here is Tall-Tale Night at my place, and I am prepared to believe anything you can say with a straight face. Hell, I sometimes believe the Doc over there, and his face ain't never been straight. Come on, spit it out. Maybe you won't owe me for them sandwiches and beer after all." The big Irishman put a fresh light on his everpresent El Ropo and gave the kid a fresh beer to lube his mouth with.

I looked around; the boys were reverting to their favorite listening postures as naturally and gracefully as Paladin used to go into that gunfighter's crouch of his. *The hell with the budget,* I decided, and slapped another single on the bar, helping myself to a shot of Irish uisgebagh from the bottle labeled, "Give Every Man His Dew."

"It started with my brother Paul," MacDonald began, and I groaned inside. The perfect shaggy-relative story, shot to hell. "He was ten years older than me, and he was really only my half-brother. Dad divorced and remarried when Paul was only three, and that's why I had some hope for a while.

"You see, Paul was a mutant.

"Not in any gross physical sense—his body was not malformed in any detectable way. But he was an Instantaneous Echo.

"You've probably heard of them, maybe seen one on T.V. or read about 'em in places like Charles Fort. From the age of twelve Paul could mimic anything you said—at the instant that you said it. The voice and inflection were different, but he never stumbled, even when he didn't comprehend the words he was parroting. No noticeable time-lag—he simply said what you were saying, as you said it. Sometimes he actually seemed to jump the gun by a hair, and *that* was really strange.

Around the time that I was five, a couple of fellows from Duke came around with a truck-full of equipment and put Paul through a series of tests. At first they were quite excited, but as the testing continued their excitement wore off, and eventually they told my father that Paul was just like all the other Instant Echoes they'd studied, simply a man who'd learned how to hook his mouth in parallel with his ears. According to their newest findings, he could not in fact "jump the gun" as he sometimes seemed to, and while the actual lag was small, they claimed to be able to measure it. They were unhappy. They'd hoped to prove that Paul was a telepath.

"Me, I think he got cagey.

"Paul had always been an introspective kid and about that time he became moodier than ever. He seldom left the house, and when he did he was quite likely to return in tears, claiming a migraine as the cause. My father got our doctor to prescribe some strong stuff for the migraines, but it didn't seem to help for too long. Paul, having finished high school at fifteen with excellent grades, showed no interest whatever in college, a job or girls. He seemed to be the typical loner, with a bit of hypochondria thrown in.

"It was about then that the trouble started between my father and mother (Paul's stepmother, you understand). She felt that Paul had to earn a living regardless of his headaches, and insisted that he should do so at sideshows and on nightclub stages, doing his instant echo routine. Dad was having none of it; he'd made a good deal of money with a good deal of hard work, running a used-car

chain, but he was perfectly willing to indulge a tempera-
mentally infirm son, rather than set him on a stage to be
gawked at by yokels. Mother was . . . not a very nice
person, I'm afraid, and I suspect she thought of the child
she had inherited as an untapped gold mine scant years
from his majority. I think she wanted Paul to make a
bundle while she could still get at it; she'd always had
some of the Backstage Mother Complex. How I managed
to remain neutral I don't know. But then, nobody asked
my opinion.

"When Paul was twenty and I was nine and a half, I got
my first big scare.

"It was all an accident, for by this time Paul had
become uncannily adept at avoiding people, leaving the
house only after dark and never straying far. The only spot
he showed any affection for was the abandoned gravel pit
a few miles from home, a place so gloomy at night that
even the area's love-struck teenagers avoided it. I went
there with him two or three times—Paul seemed to accept
my company more often than anyone else's, particularly
when I was younger. I didn't especially care for the place
myself—it seemed to me the loneliest place I'd ever
imagined—but I suppose a kid will follow his big brother
just about anywhere he's invited.

"I think that must be where he met the girl.

"Mom and Dad were out that night at a P.T.A. meeting
or some such. I was watching T.V., and if you want to
know the truth, I was eating some stolen jelly beans from
the horde Mother used to hide away for herself. So when
Paul came crashing through the front door, I jumped a foot
in the air before I even saw him. When I got downstairs,
my first crazy thought was that the migraines had finally
split poor Paulie's head open. He looked . . . well, I
guess I've given you a pretty fair imitation tonight, crashing in here the way I did. His scalp was laid open around
the sides of his head, his forehead was dripping blood in

lines that streamed crazily over his face, his fingers were raw and bleeding, and his eyes held so much agony that even at nine years old I was more terrified by them than by anything else.

"He was babbling incoherently, swinging his arms wildly as if to ward off some closing demon, and sobbing as though his heart would break. I'd never seen anyone his age cry like that, you know? I rushed to his side and got him to sit down, and without thinking about it I went to the bar and mixed him a martini, just as Mother had taught me to do for her. Little enough of it went down his throat, but it calmed him some, and the rest at least got some of the blood off his chin.

"Of course, when he'd calmed down a little I asked him what had happened. 'She looked so nice, Jimmy,' he raved, 'so *nice*. I thought it would be all right. I mean, I knew it would be bad, but I thought I could take it. *She looked so god damned nice,*' he shrieked, trembling like a leaf. Finally I got the story out of him in bits and pieces.

"It seems my brother was a telepath, after all.

"A latent telepath, at any rate. From age five to fifteen, his only telepathic manifestation was his instant-echo bit, and that was done unconsciously. Subvocalized thoughts must be closest to the surface. During that time he never received thoughts except those about to be verbalized, never sensed emotions, and never had any conscious volitional control of his wild talent.

"But about midway through puberty the picture began to change. His power was still beyond his control, but it *grew*. With no warning, he would suddenly find himself inside someone else's head, with increasing frequency and for increasing lengths of time. The first time he plugged in was for a split-second only, just enough to scare him silly, and it didn't reoccur for a couple of months. By now, he told me, telepathy came to him every week or so, for as much as five or ten minutes at a time.

"You must understand, this was nothing like the traditional 'telepathy' of science-fiction stories. It was not the ability to send messages without speech; Paul had never succeeded in sending anything. Nor was it the ability to receive such messages. It was, rather, a process of entering the skull of another, receiving its entire contents and preceiving them as a gestalt.

"I wonder if you can imagine what that's like? Perhaps, if you've ever thought of telepathy at all, you've thought of how terrible it would be if someone were inside your strongest defenses, privy to all your secrets and desires and shameful memories and frustrated lusts and true feelings. Well you might—but have you ever considered how terrible it would be to find yourself in someone *else's* head, with all that unsought and unwanted knowledge? As long as people remain locked in their own skulls, they should be—because as most people intuitively realize, the things that grow and fester in a sealed skull aren't always fit to share.

"On top of that, there's the sheer shock of directly confronting a naked ego as strong as your own, and Paul told me that night that it doesn't help a bit that the other ego is unaware of you. Most people never get over believing that they're the center of the Universe, even when they know it isn't so—to have your nose rubbed in it is unsettling.

"And so, Paul told me between sobs, he began avoiding people the best he could as his strange and terrifying power grew in him. Repeated exposure made the minds of his immediate family tolerable to him, and his telepathy seemed to be sharply limited by distance, with an effective radius of about a hundred feet or so. By keeping strangers beyond that limit, Paul could achieve peace of a sort, the flashes of telepathy bringing him only glimpses of Dad, Mother and myself. Dad he pitied with an intensity heretofore unknown to that emotion; Mother he hated

beyond all understanding; and me he often found sooth-
ing, until I grew up enough to start having dark secrets of
my own. He told me some things about myself then, that
. . . but that's irrelevant.

"The point is, that night, communing with himself in
the moonlit gravel pit, he met a girl, about his age or a little
older. One of the strange things about out-of-the-way
places is that, while you almost never meet anyone there,
anyone you do run into is somehow very liable to be
friend-material. At any rate, she seemed to Paul the nicest
and most gentle girl he'd ever seen in his life, not at all like
any other girl he'd ever met. She spoke softly, and only
when she had something to say, and he felt in her a
difference that he could not explain to me in words.

"Whatever the reason, he let down his guard for once.
Instead of running away or driving her from him with
rudeness, as he had learned to do with strangers, he stayed
to talk. Before too many minutes had passed, he began to
lose the usual terrifying fear that his wild talent would
strike, began to believe that it might be all right if it did,
began finally to amost hope that it would.

"And it did.

"I'm sure she was a lovely girl, but the best of us harbor
dark secrets—sometimes even from ourselves. I don't
know specifically what shattered Paul that night, but I'm
sure it was nothing that a bishop on his deathbed would
have felt compelled to confess. Maybe it was nothing
more dishonorable than her lifetime's accumulation of
pain, for one's own sorrow may be bearable by its famil-
iarity and yet staggering to a stranger.

"In any event, it hit Paul even harder than usual,
because he had dared to hope. Now, if your ears are
overloaded, you can stuff your fingers into them; if your
nose is outraged, you can hold it; if your eyes are blinded
you can shield them with your arm. But when you brain
itself is overwhelmed by direct input, all you can do is

smash at it with a rock, hoping to drive the other consciousness away with your own. Sometimes, if you're lucky, it works.

"For Paul, that night, it hadn't worked.

"Now you must understand that I was very young. I barely comprehended the things that Paul was telling me, and if I understood what had happened, I surely didn't understand why it had hit him as hard as it obviously had. Being able to read minds had no drawback that my nine-year-old mind could see; I sure didn't know much about human nature. But I was trying hard to empathize with my big brother.

"That's the only explanation I have for what occurred. Because as Paul reached the terrible climax of his story, for one split second a shutter opened—and like a camera plate, my child's mind was imprinted with the total contents of the mind of my brother.

"It lasted only that split second, and it faded about as fast as a flashbulb-burst from two feet away; the impact was over quickly, but the blinding afterimage seared my brain for many seconds more. I screamed. Several times. Instantly our positions were reversed, and Paulie was holding me, restraining my hands. He knew at once what had happened, and the grim set of his jaw said that he had been expecting it for years now.

" 'It's over,' he barked, 'Jimmy listen to me, it's over. It won't happen again for months, maybe years.'

"It wasn't what he said but the pure joyous relief of how *far away* his voice sounded that cut through my child's terror and brought me back from the edge of hysteria. Why, Paulie was *miles* away—at least a foot! And there were comforting walls of bone, cartilage and skin—and blessed empty air!—between us. I calmed down, and Paulie held me tightly in his arms and in savage whispers explained to me what I was, what had happened to us, and what I could expect from now on. He had hoped, he said, that I would be spared because my maternal genes were different from his; he explained genetics to me, as well as it can be explained to a nine-year-old, and he told me what a mutant was. He told me how much easier to bear the telepathic flashes would become, and he told me how much easier they would not become. He told me how often to expect the onslaught ('flashing,' he called it), and advised me on how to avoid flashing by avoiding sentient beings as much as possible. I suppose you could say it was the end of my childhood. I know that four years later, when my father haltingly undertook to explain the Facts of Life to me, they came as a helluvan anticlimax.

"I suppose that next landmark in the story is the night my father and I found Paul collapsed across my mother in the living room, the lamp that had crushed her skull still clenched in his hand, but I don't think I want to talk about that now. They took Paul away that night, like a sack of sugar, and hauled him off to King's Park, completely catatonic. He's been that way ever since, and as far as I can tell he never flashed again. Or anything.

"That was fourteen years ago."

Callahan had been refilling his glass as he talked, but MacDonald spilled this one over half the table. He drank the rest as fast as it could pour and shut up.

"I get it," Fast Eddie said after a while. "Yer afraid de same t'ing is gonna happen ta you."

"Jesus," Doc Webster said in an undertone behind me, "he's just about due." I did some rapid mental calculation, and turned pale.

"No, Eddie," I said aloud. "Jim's overdue. Unless . . ." I let it trail off.

MacDonald grinned hideously, shook his head. "No, friend, I haven't killed anyone yet . . . though I wouldn't care to make any predictions for tomorrow. No, my pattern didn't follow Paul's after all. Not precisely, that is. For one thing, I never was an instant echo.

"I waited all through adolescence for the next flash, and when it hadn't come by the time I graduated high school I dared to begin to hope that I was different. By sophomore year of college, I'd shoved the fear back into the far corners of my mind, and convinced myself that my one fleeting experience had been a freak, perhaps Paul sending instead of receiving for once.

"In Junior year it hit again, in the middle of a party. I was paralyzed. There were *twenty-one people* there, and for one awful second I was sure my head would burst from overcrowding. I learned more about human nature that night than I had in the previous twenty years, and I very nearly died. I passed out eventually, but not before I'd gained an undeserved reputation as an acid-head, and lost my girlfriend.

"From that point on, they started coming again and again. The next flash was six months later, the next four and a half, then five, then three, then I stopped keeping track. Right now I'd guess they hit every day or so, but I'm not sure. I can't tell you an awful lot about the time between them." His head dropped.

"Why do you suppose your pattern was different from your brother's, Jim?" Doc Webster asked.

"I'm not sure," MacDonald repeated without looking up. "Maybe the different heredity, maybe random chance."

"Perhaps," I put in, "it was getting your first jolt so much younger than Paul did. Maybe the trauma hit you so young you hadn't come to accept limits on your mind yet, and your subconscious whipped up some kind of defense that lasted as long as the trauma did."

"Maybe so," MacDonald said, glancing up at me with hopeless eyes. "But if it did, it's forgotten how to do it

again. And my conscious doesn't know the trick." He
giggled. "I haven't even improved on Paul's trick with the
rock." The giggle dissolved into hysterical laughter, the
table danced, and his glass shattered on the floor.

Callahan's broad hand caught him open-palm across the
cheek, rocking him in his chair. His laughter cut off, and
his shoulders slumped for a second. Then he sat up very
straight and stuck his hand out soberly. Callahan shook it
gravely and produced a full glass of beer from nowhere;
MacDonald took a grateful sip.

"I suppose I should say, 'Thank you, I needed that,'
Mister . . . uh . . ."

Callahan told him his name.

". . . Mr. Callahan, but to tell you the truth I almost
think I'd rather do it myself." He looked around at the rest
of us and his face went all to pieces and he buried his head
in his arms. "Oh, *Jesus!*"

"Listen, Jim," Tommy Janssen spoke up quickly,
"what the hell did you do after that party? I mean, dig, you
couldn't stay in school, right? Too many people, flip you
right out. What did you do, go home and become a loner
like Paul?"

MacDonald spoke listlessly. "I tried, brother, I tried. I
went home and told my father everything—why his second wife had died, and what Paul was, and what I was
—and that night he got up to get a drink of water and
dropped dead in the bathroom.

"Thank God I didn't flash that.

"I got out fast after that—I got a flash of the man who
ran the funeral home that almost did make me a murderer.
So I took off, and got myself the only job I was suited
for."

"Lighthouse?" Chuck Samms guessed.

"Nope. No openings; there almost never are. But the
Forestry Service can always use fire-lookouts who don't
mind isolation. Miles from anybody in a well-stocked

cabin with nothing to do but watch the forest spread out below you. I even got lucky; the area I drew averaged thirty-five days of rain every summer, so I got to sleep late a lot. On hot days in Oregon you get to stand a twelve-hour watch.

"God, it was peaceful." He was talking freely now. "I think I got a flash from a bear once, but it must have been at the extreme limit of my range. Then one day I flashed a bluejay as it sailed about six feet over my head, and that was . . . just beautiful!" He shivered. "Almost worth the rest of it."

"What brings you this way?" Callahan wanted to know.

"What else? The expected: a forest fire in my zone. Called it in fast, and then got too close to a firefighter who was trapped by a widowmaker and roasting slowly. My boss figured me for an epileptic and fired me as gently as he could. I didn't argue the point. I had a little money saved up. I came back east."

"Why? Callahan asked.

"To see Paul. To visit him."

"Have you?"

"No, damn it, I couldn't get near the place. I flew right into MacArthur, doped up with sleeping pills so I'd be asleep when we went over New York City, and rented a car with the last of my bankroll when I landed. I intended to drive on through and hope for the best, but halfway out of Islip I flashed a guy in the next lane. He . . . he was a drug dealer: Heroin and cocaine."

Tommy Janssen's face went hard as a rock, and he gripped his beermug like a bludgeon.

"I was very, very lucky," MacDonald continued. "Any crash you walk away from is a good one, and that's what I did: just left the wreck married to a tree, climbed up the embankment and walked away. I walked for *hours*, and not too long ago the supervisor of this town we're in drove past me in his big limousine and I flashed him. The next thing I knew I was in here, talking a blue streak. Hey, how come you guys believe all this?"

We looked around at each other, shrugged. "Dis here is Callahan's Place," Fast Eddie tried to explain, and somehow MacDonald seemed to understand.

"Anyway," he sent on, "that's the whole story. King's Park is a long way from here, and frankly, gentlemen, I don't think I can make it any further. Any suggestions?"

There was a long silence.

Fast Eddie opened his mouth, closed it, opened it again and left it that way. Shorty scratched where it itched. Doc Webster sipped thoughtfully at his drink. I racked my brains.

Callahan spoke. "One."

MacDonald started, turned to face him. He looked Callahan up and down from his thinning red hair to his outsized brogans, and sat up a little straighter. "I would very much like to hear it, Mr. Callahan," he said respectfully.

"Contact Paul from here," Callahan said flatly.

MacDonald shook his head violently. "I *can't*. I told you, this thing can't be controlled, dammit."

"You said 'no' a little too loud, old son," Callahan grinned. "Maybe you can't do it—but you think you can."

MacDonald shook his head again. "No. I don't want to flash him. Don't you understand? He's catatonic. A vegetable. I just want to see him, to try and speak with him."

"Why use words?" I asked.

"They're less dangerous, damn you," he snapped. "If you fail with words you can say to yourself, 'Gee, that's sad,' and go do something else."

"What else?" Doc asked. "What did you plan to do after you saw Paul?"

"I . . . I don't know."

"Well, then."

"Look, what could it possibly accomplish?" Mac-Donald barked.

"Maybe a lot," Callahan said quietly. "Here's how I figure: Paul found a way to block the flashes out—a defense. But he found it at the end of his rope—so he just threw it up and slapped ferrocement over it, and he's been huddling inside it ever since." Callahan took the cigar out of his mouth and rubbed his granite jaw. "Now you're in sorry shape, but old son I don't judge you to be at the end of your rope yet. Paul was continuously telepathic by the time he killed his stepmother, wasn't he?"

"Yes, I believe he was," MacDonald admitted. He was thinking hard.

"Well, there you are. If you can reach him, remind him of what it's like to be hooked into reality without flashing, maybe you can talk him into coming out from behind that shield, and using it only when he needs it. In return, maybe he can teach you how to build the shield.

"What do you say, son?"

MacDonald grimaced. "I can't flash at will. The distance is too great. Our maximum fields of sensitivity don't reach each other by several miles. I'm not due to flash again for at least a day or two, and Paul . . . doesn't flash any more."

"All right," Callahan agreed. "Those are the reasons why it can't possibly work. Now, why don't you try it?"

"Because I'm afraid, dammit!"

Doc Webster spoke up softly. "No reason to fret, son. We'll keep you from hurting yourself."

MacDonald looked around at us, started to speak and paused. His eyes were terrible to see.

"That's not what scares me," he admitted at last, in a voice like a murdered hope. "What scares me is that I may establish contact with my brother and *not* be able to kill myself.''

Callahan lumbered around behind the bar, brought his shotgun from beneath it and laid it on the bar-top.

"Son," he said firmly, "I don't like violence in my joint. And suicide usually strikes me as a coward's solution. But if you need to die, I'll see that you do."

A couple of jaws dropped, but nobody objected.

Except MacDonald. "What about the police?"

"That's my problem, burglar."

MacDonald's eyes seemed to see a far place, and I hope to God I never see it myself. I suppose he was examining his guts. The suspense hung in the air like the electric calm before a cyclone, and nobody made a sound.

After a long, timeless moment he nodded faintly. "All right. I'll try, Mr. Callahan."

We relaxed a trifle in our chairs, and then tensed right back up again. Callahan put out his cigar and laid a hand on the shotgun, unobtrusively waving Chuck and Noah out of the line of fire.

MacDonald sat bolt upright, put his hands over his ears. He opened his eyes real wide, looked around one last time, and closed them tight. His brow knotted up.

Now, I don't know quite how to explain just what happened next, because it doesn't seem to jibe with what Jim MacDonald had told us. But I figure that if he was a telepath, some of us at Callahan's are pretty fair empaths. Maybe he was tapping us himself, maybe not. All I know for sure is that all at once the lights were gone and I wasn't in the bar any more, and Callahan and the Doc and Fast Eddie and Tommy and Long-Drink and Noah and Shorty and Chuck and I were all crowded together somehow, *touching*, like we were rubbing shoulders in back of a truck we had to push-start. We didn't waste time wondering, we put our backs into it.

That's crazy, there was no truck, not even a hallucinatory one, but I guess it describes the sort of thing we did as well as words can. We . . . *pushed,* and just like with a truck there came a time when the thing we were pushing gave a hell of a shudder and took off, leaving us gasping far behind.

The thing we were pushing was Jim MacDonald.

The lights came back and the familiar sights of Callahan's Place came back and I was alone in my skin again, looking around at Callahan and the rest of the boys and realizing with surprise that I hadn't been the least bit scared. They were looking around too, and it was a few seconds before we saw MacDonald.

He was sitting rigid in his chair, trembling like a man with a killing fever. Doc Webster started for him like an overweight white corpuscle but pulled up short and looked helpless. The air around MacDonald's head seemed to shimmer like the air over a campfire, and we heard his teeth gnashing.

Then, not suddenly but gradually, almost imperceptibly at first, he began to relax. Muscles unknotted, joints unlocked, his face began to soften. He . . . I don't know how to say this either. He *wore his face differently.* The MacDonald he loosened into was changed, somehow older.

He had won.

"Our deepest thanks, gentlemen," he said in a more resonant voice than he had used before. "I think we'll be all right from here on."

"What will you do now?" Callahan rapped, and I wondered at the cold steel in his voice.

MacDonald considered for a moment. "We're not really sure," he decided finally, "but whatever we do, we hope we can find a way to help other people the way you've helped us. There must be lots of things we can do. Maybe we'll finish school and become a psychiatrist like I planned once. Imagine—a telepathic headshrinker.''

Callahan's hand came away from the trigger of the scattergun for the first time; Jim/Paul didn't catch it, but I did. I was rather glad to know that the intentions of the world's only two telepaths were benign, myself.

Callahan looked puzzled for a second, then his face split into a huge grin. "Say, can I offer you fellas a drink?"

And MacDonald's new voice echoed him perfectly.

"Don't mind if we do," he added, laughing, and got up to take a chair at the bar.

"Hey," Fast Eddie called out, ever one to remember the important details, "wait a minute. De cops'll be lookin' for youse fer leavin' dat accident. Whaddya gonna tell 'em? Fer dat matter, how d'ya get yer udder body outa King's Park?''

"Oh, I dunno," Callahan mused, putting a careful double-shot of Chivas Regal in front of MacDonald. "It seems to me a telepath could dodge him a lot of cops. Or a lot of witchdoctors. Wouldn't you say, gents?"

"We guess so," MacDonald allowed, and drank up.

And they were right. All three of them.

I haven't heard much from either of the MacDonald brothers yet, but then it hasn't been that long, and I'm sure they've both got a lot of thinking and catching up to do. I wonder if either of them is thinking of having kids. One way or another, I expect to be hearing good things of them, really good things, any day now.

It figures. I mean, two heads are better than one.

5

The Law of Conservation of Pain

There's a curious kind of inevitability to the way things happen at Callahan's. Not that we wouldn't have managed to help The Meddler out *some* way or other even if it had been, say, Thursday night that he came to us. But since it was Monday night, I finally got to learn what it is that "heavy-metal" rock music is good for.

After ten years as a musician, it was about time I found out.

Monday night is Fill-More Night at Callahan's Place, the night Fast Eddie and I do our weekly set on piano and guitar. But don't let the name mislead you into thinking we play the kind of ear-splitting music the Fillmore East was famous for. Although I do play an electric axe (a Country Gent Six) and have an amplifier factory-guaranteed to shatter glass, these are the only remnants of a very brief flirtation with heavy-metal that occurred in much hungrier times than these. I don't *like* loud noises.

No, the name derives from the curious custom we have at Callahan's of burying our dead soldiers in the fireplace. You can usually tell how good a night it's been by how many glasses lay smashed on the hearth, and after one particularly tasty session Doc Webster nicknamed Eddie and me the Fireside Fill-More. To our intense disgust, it stuck.

This particular Monday night, things was loose indeed. Eddie and I had held off our first set for half an hour to accommodate a couple of the boys who were playing a sort of pool on the floor with apples and broomsticks, and by the time Callahan had set up the two immense speakers on either side of the front door, the joint was pretty merry.

"What're you gonna play, Jake?" the Doc called out from his ringside seat. I adjusted the mikestand, turned up my axe just enough to put it on an equal footing with Fast Eddie's upright, and tossed the ball right back to the Doc.

"What would you like to hear, Doc?"

"How about, 'There Are Tears In My Ears From Lying On My Back And Crying In The Evening Over You?' "

"Naw," drawled Long-Drink from the bar, "I want to hear 'He Didn't Like Her Apartment So He Knocked Her Flat,' " and a few groans were heard.

Doc Webster rose to the occasion. "Why not play the Butcher Song, Jake?"

I resigned myself to the inevitable. "The Butcher Song?"

"Sure," boomed the Doc, and conducting an invisible band, he sang, "Butcher arms around me honey/hold me tight . . ." Peanuts began to rain on his head.

Callahan shifted the right speaker a bit, and turned around with his hands on his hips. "Play the Camera Song, Jake."

"Hit me, Mike."

With a voice like a fog-horn undergoing root-canal work, Callahan began, "Lens get together 'bout half past eight/I'll ring your Bell & Howell . . ." and a considerable number of glasses hit the fireplace at once. One or two had not been emptied first; the crackling fire flared high.

In the brief pause that ensued, Fast Eddie spoke up plaintively.

"Hey Jake. I got an idea."

"Be gentle with it," the Doc grinned. "It's in a strange place."

"What's your idea, Eddie?" I asked.

"How about if we do de one we been rehoisin' all afternoon?"

I nodded judiciously, and turned to face the house. "Regulars and gentlemen," I announced, "for our first number we would like to do a song we wrote yesterday in an attempt to define that elusive essence, that shared quality which brings us all together here at Callahan's Place. In its way it is a song about all of us.

"It's called the Drunkard's Song."

And as Eddie's nimble piano intro cut through the ensuing catcalls, I stoked up my guitar and sang:

> A swell and wealthy relative of mine had up and died
> And I got a hundred thousand from the will
> So a friend and I decided to convert it into liquid form
> The better our esophagi to fill
> So we started in the city, had a drink in every shitty
> Little ginmill, which is really quite a few
> And a cabbie up in Harlem took us clean across the river
> Into Brooklyn, where he joined us in a brew
> We was weavin' just a trifle as we pulled into Astoria
> At eighty miles an hour in reverse
> But it was nothin' to the weavin' that we did as we was leavin'
> And from time to time it got a little worse
>> Well there's nothin' like drinkin' up a windfall
>> We was drunker than a monkey with a skinfull
>> We wuz so goddam drunk it was sinful
>> And I think I ain't sober yet

As we finished the chorus, Fast Eddie tossed up a cloud of gospel chords that floated me easily into my solo, a bit of intricate pickin' which I managed to stumble through with feeling if not precision. When it was Eddie's turn I snuck a look around and saw that everyone was well into his second drink, and relaxed. There were smiles all around as I slid into the second verse:

> We was feeling mighty fine as we crossed the city line
> Suckin' whiskey and a-whistlin' at the girls
> But the next saloon we try someone wants to black my eye
> 'Cause he doesn't like my brown and shaggy curls
> So then a fist come out of orbit, knocked me clean across the floor
> But I was pretty drunk and didn't even care
> And I was pretty disappointed when the coppers hit the joint
> As I was makin' my rebuttal with a chair
> But the coppers came a cropper 'cause I made it to the crapper
> And departed by a ventilator shaft
> Met my buddies in the alley as they slipped out through the galley
> And we ran and ran and laughed and laughed and laughed
>> Yeah there's nothin' like drinkin' up a windfall
>> We was drunker than a monkey with a skinful
>> We wuz so goddam drunk it was sinful
>> And I think I ain't sober yet

This time Fast Eddie jumped into the gap with a flurry of triplets. I could tell that he knew where he was going, so I gave him his head. As he unfolded a tasty statement, I looked around again and saw all-to-wall grins again.

No, not quite. Tommy Janssen, sitting over by the mixer, was definitely not smiling. A pot-bellied gent in an overcoat, who I didn't recognize, was leaning over Tommy's shoulder, whispering something into his ear, and the kid didn't seem to like it at all. Even as Eddie's solo yanked my attention away again I saw Tommy turn around and say something to the overcoated man, and when I looked back the guy was standing at the bar with his nose in a double-something.

I put it out of my mind; verse three was a-comin'.

Halfway out of Levittown we got our second wind
In a joint so down it made you laugh
So I had another mug, and my buddy had a jug
And the cabbie had a pitcher and a half
When we got to Suffolk County we was goin' into
*   overdrive*
The word had spread and crowds began to form
We drank our way from Jericho on down 110 to
*   Merrick Road*
A-boozin' and a-singin' up a storm
I lost my buddy and the cabbie in the middle of the
*   Hamptons*
We was drunker than it's possible to be
But there finally came a time when I just didn't have a
*   dime*
I sat on Montauk Point and wept into the sea

And everybody in the joint joined in on the final chorus. All except the guy in the overcoat . . . who was already on his second double-something.

Yeah there's nothin' like drinkin' up a windfall
We was drunker than a monkey with a skinfull
We wuz so goddam drunk it was sinful
*   And I think I ain't sober yet!*

A storm of glasses hit the fireplace, and Fast Eddie and I went into our aw-shucks routine at about the same time. When the cheers and laughter had died down somewhat, I stepped back up to the mike and a-hemmed.

"Thank you for your sympathy, genties and ladle-men," I said. "We'll be passing the eleven-gallon hat directly." I tapped the huge Stetson on my head significantly and grinned.

"Well now . . ." I paused. "We only know two songs, and that was one of them, so we're real glad you liked it." I stopped again. "What dn you think we ought to play now, Eddie?"

He sat awhile in thought.

"How 'bout de udder one?" he asked at last.

"Right arm," I agreed at once, and hit a G.

Doc Webster beheaded a new bottle of Peter Dawson's and took a hearty swallow.

"Okay, folks," I continued. "Here's a medley of our hit: a sprightly number called, 'She Was Only A Telegrapher's Daughter, But She Didit-Ah-Didit.' " I started to pick the intro, but the sound of glass smashing in the fireplace distracted me, and I bungled it.

And in the few seconds before I could take another stab at it, the fellow in the overcoat burst noisily and explosively into tears.

Fast Eddie and I were among the first to join the circle that formed immediately around the crying, pot-bellied man. I didn't even stop to unplug my guitar, and if anyone had trouble stepping over the stretched-out telephone cord they kept it to themselves.

Paradoxically, after we had rushed to encircle him, nobody said a word. We let him have his cry, and did our best to silently share it with him. We offered him only our presence, and our concern.

In about five minutes, his sobs gave way to grimaces and jerky breathing, and Callahan handed him a triple-something. He got outside of half of it at once, and set the remaining something-and-a-half down on the bar. His face as he looked around us was not ashamed, as we might have expected; more relieved than anything else. Although there was still tension in the set of his lantern jaw and in the squint of his hazel eyes, the know in his gut seemed to have eased considerably.

"Thanks," he said quietly. "I . . . I . . . ." He stopped, wanting to talk about it but unable to continue. Then he must have remembered the few toasts he'd seen earlier in the evening, because he picked up the rest of his drink, walked over to the chalk line in the middle of the room, drained the glass and announced, "To meddlers." Then he pegged the glass into the exact geometrical center of the fireplace.

"Like me," he added, turning to face us. "I'm a meddler on a grand scale, and I'm not sure I've got the guts. Or the right."

"Brother," Callahan said seriously, "you're sure in the right place. All of us here are veteran meddlers, after a fashion, and we worry considerable about both them things."

"Not like this," the Meddler said. "You see, I'm a time-traveler too." He waited for our reaction.

"Say," piped up Noah Gonzalez, "it's a shame Tom Hauptman's off tonight. You two'd have a lot to talk about."

"Eh?" said the stranger, confused.

"Sure," Callahan agreed. "Tom's a time-traveler too."

"But . . . but," the guy sputtered, "but I've got the only unit."

"Oh, Tom didn't use no fancy equipment," Noah explained.

"Yeah," agreed Callahan. "Tom did it the hard way. Never mind, friend, it's a long story. You from the past or the future?"

"The future," said the time-traveler, puzzled at our

lack of reaction. I guess we're hard to startle. "That is, the future as it is at present . . . I mean . . ." He stopped and looked confused.

"I get it," said Noah, like me a veteran SF fan. "You're from the future, but you're going to change that future by changing the past, which is our present, right?"

The fellow nodded.

"How's that again?" blinked Doc Webster.

"I am from the year 1995," said ths man in the overcoat with weary patience, "and I am going to change history in the year 1974. If I succeed, the world I go back to will be different from the one I left."

"Better or worse?" asked Callahan.

"That's the hell of it: I don't know. Oh kark, I might as well tell you the whole story. Maybe it'll help."

Callahan set 'em up, and we all got comfortable.

Her name (said the stranger) was Bobbi Joy, and you couldn't say there'd never been anyone like her before. Lots of people had been like her. April Lawton, for instance, was nearly as good a guitarist. Aretha had at times a similar intensity. Billie Holiday surely bore and was able to communicate much the same kind of pain. Joni Mitchell and Roberta Flack each in their own way possessed a comparable technical control and purity of tone. Dory Previn was as dramatic and poignant a lyricist, and Maria Muldaur projected the same artless grace.

But you could have rolled them all together and you still wouldn't have Bobbi Joy, because there was her voice. And it was just plain impossible that such a voice could be. When a Bobbi Joy song ended, whether on tape or disc or holo or, rarest of good fortune, live, you found your head shaking in frank disbelief that a human throat could express such pain, that such pain could be, and that you could hear such pain and still live.

Her name was the purest of irony, given to her by an employer in a previous and more ancient profession, a name she was too cynically indifferent to change when her first recordings began to sell. I've often wondered what her past customers must feel when they hear her sing; I'm certain every nameless, faceless one of them remembers *her*.

They surely appreciate as well as anyone the paradox of her name—for while God seemed to have given her every possible physical advantage in obtaining joy, it never got any closer to her than her album jackets and the first line of her driver's license. Although many pairs of lips spoke her name, none ever brought its reality to her.

For the scar on her soul was as deep and as livid as the one that ran its puckered, twisted way from her left cheekbone to her right chin.

The Woman With The Scar, they called her, and many, seeing only a physical wound, might have wondered that she did not have it surgically corrected—so easy a procedure in my time. But she sang, and so we understood, and we cried with her because neither of her scars would or could ever be erased, and that, I suppose you'd say, was her genius. She represented the scars across the face of an entire era; she reminded us that we had made the world in which such scars could be, and that we—all of us—were as scarred as she. She . . .

This is absurd. I'm trying to explain sex to a virgin, with a perfectly good bed handy. Lend an ear, friends, and listen. This holo will tell you more than I can. God help you.

The stranger produced a smooth blue sphere about the size of a tennis ball from one of his pockets, and held it out toward the fireplace. The shimmering of the air over the crackling fire intensified and became a swirling, then a dancing, and finally a coalescing. The silence in Callahan's was something you could have driven rivets into.

Then the fireplace was gone, and in its place was a young black woman seated on a rock, a guitar on her lap and starry night sky all around and behind her. Her face was in shadow, but even as we held our breath the moon came out from behind a cloud and touched her features. It gave an obsidian sheen to her skin, a tender softness to a face that God had meant to be beautiful, and made a harsh shadow-line of the incredibly straight slash that began an inch below her left eye and yanked sideways and down to open up lips that had been wide already, like a jagged black underline below the word "pain." She was black and a woman and scarred, and as the thought formed in our minds we realized that it was a redundancy. Her scar was visible externally, was all.

We were shocked speechless, and in the stillness she lifted her guitar slightly and began to play, a fast, nagging, worrisome beat, like despairing Richie Havens, an unresolved and maybe unresolvable chord that was almost all open string. An E minor sixth, with the C sharp in the bass, a haunting chord that demanded to become something else, major or minor, happy or sad, but *something*. A plain, almost Gregorian riff began from that C sharp but always returned unsatisfied, trying to break free of that chord but not succeeding.

And over that primevally disturbing sound, Bobbi Joy spoke, with the impersonal tones of the narrator behind all art:

Snow was falling heavily on U.S. 40 as the day drew to a close. This lonely stretch of highway had seen no other movement all day; the stillness was so complete that the scrub pines and rolling hills by the roadside may have felt that the promise given them so long ago had come to pass, that man had finally gone and left them in peace forever. No snakes had swayed forth from their retreats that day, no lizards crawled, no wolves padded silently in search of winter food. All wildlife waited, puzzled, expectant, caught in the feeling of waiting . . . for what?

Gradually, without suddenness, each living thing became aware of a curious stuttering drone to the far east, which became audible too slowly to startle. It swelled, drew nearer, and small muscles and sinews tensed, then relaxed as the sound was identified as familiar, harmless.

A pale green 1960 Dodge, with no more than three cylinders firing, crept jerkily into view through the shrouds of snow. Wipers blinking clumsily, the great machine felt its way along the road, its highway song hoarse and stuttered. With a final roar of mortal agony, it fell silent: wipers ceased their wiping, pistons ceased driving, lights winked out, and the huge car coasted gracefully off the road and rolled to a stop with its nose resting on a snow-laden mesquite.

Stillness returned to U.S. 40 . . . and still, on either side of it, the animals waited.

Even as she finished speaking, the walking bass line with which she was underpinning her mournful chord returned to that dysharmonic C sharp. Then with breathtaking ease it slid down two tones to B, became the dominant of a simple E minor, and as bass, organ and drums came in from nowhere she began to sing:

Snow fallin' gentle on the windshield
Sittin' on the side of the road
Took a ride—my engine died and left me
Sittin' on the side of the road
In a little while I'll get out and start a-walkin'
Probably a town pretty near
But it just occurs to me that I ain't got no
More reason to be there than to be here

> *But I'll be leavin'*
> (sudden key shift)
>> *Soon as I find me a reason to*
>> *Right now it's nice just to watch the snow*
>> *Coverin' the windshield and windows . . .*

She finished on a plaintive A minor, toppled off it back into that ghostly mosquito-biting E minor sixth again, and the other instruments fell away, leaving her guitar alone. Again, she spoke:

> *Snow now completely covered the windshield and windows, forming a white curtain which hid the interior of the car, and any activity within—if there was any to be seen. No sound issued from the car, no vibration disturbed the snow on its doors. The animals were puzzled, but delighted: perhaps a human understood at last.*

The C sharp walked down to B again, but this time it belonged to a clean, simple G chord, supported by a steel guitar and the trapping of bluegrass, a comparatively happy sound that only lasted for the first four lines as that voice—that voice!—picked up the song again, etching us with its words:

> *Don't worry now. I'm goin'*
> *Any minute now, I'll be goin'*
> *Leave the car*
> *—It isn't far to walk now*
> *Any minute now, I'll be going*

(slowing now, an electric guitar leading into an achingly repeated C-E A-minor progression that went nowhere . . .)

> *Soon as I can find a place I want to go*
> *Soon as I can find a thing I want to do*
> *Soon as I can find someone I want to know*
> *Or think of something interesting and new*

(a sudden optimistic jump into the key of F . . .)

I mean, I could make it easy to the next town
(twisting crazily into E flat . . .)
But what am I to do when I get there?
(inexorably back to C. . .)
That's what I made this odyssey to find out:
Two thousand miles and still I just don't care . . .
(a capella:)
Is it worthwhile to go on looking?

We wanted to cry, wanted to shout, wanted to run
forward with a hundred reasons for living, find some way
to heal the hurt in that voice, and no one made a sound.
Alone again with her guitar, Bobbi Joy wove that dysharmonic tapestry of hurting notes that was already becoming
as familiar to us as the taste that a bad dream always has in
the cold morning; and as she began to speak again, not a
muscle flickered in her ebony face, as though her scar was
all the expression she would ever need or be allowed.

The snow began to drift.
In a minute—or an hour—the car was half-buried in a
heavy white winter coat of wet snow. The animals were
already beginning to forget about the car. It had not
shown movement in so long that they were coming to
regard it as part of their environment—of less interest than
the tattered 1892 edition of the Denver Record *pinned*
under a rock, which at least still fluttered occasionally in
the wind.
For the memory of the animals is short, and the years
are long, and they have found that very little is worth
puzzling over for very long.
And still, the snow fell . . .

This time she stayed with the C sharp, built an A chord
around it, and was joined only by harpsichord and bass.
There was no ambiguity to this part: a simple, mournful

melody that had no change-ups, no surprises, just the quiet
calm of resignation, of unheeded defeat.

Sort of friendly here inside the car
Even though it's gettin' kinda cold
Haven't stirred, or said a word, in hours
I believe it's gettin' awful cold
In the glove compartment, there's a small flask:
Little Irish whiskey for the soul
But reachin' out to get it seems a great task
And anyway, it isn't all that cold
It might keep me warm
But it just ain't worth the trouble . . .

Her shoulders seemed to slump, and the droning background of her guitar took on a terrible finality.

There was no longer a Dodge by the side of U.S. 40;
just a drift like many others, peaceful and horribly cold. A
faint illumination began to expose mysteries of snow-
sculpture, hummocks and valleys of white. But for the
swirling haze, you might have said it was dawn.
The car was completely hidden from sight—and so, in
caves, holes and shelters, were the animals. But they no
longer remembered the car . . . and at least in their
dwellings were some signs of life.

And with shattering unexpectedness she slammed into
E major, driving with horns and bass and moog and drums
in a frenzied hallelujah chorus that dared you to begin
hoping again. Surely that throbbing beat was a heart
starting to beat, surely that energy was purposeful!
We sat up straighter, and crossed our fingers.

I've got it!
There's something that I want to do
A thing that seems to have some kind of point
I've got some grass, enclosed in glass

Here inside my shirt
Think I'm gonna roll myself a joint
(the bottom fell out of voice and arrangement, scared
away by solemnity and a trembling echo . . .)
A complicated operation—might disturb the peace
But it ought to warm me just as well as drink
So it's something worth the trouble and it's gonna help
*   me find*
A reason to get out of here
I think
(a capella)
Now where did I put all those Zig-Zags?

Again that C sharp rang out, shocking return to inevitability, and the droning guitar cut the rug out from under us.
Helpless, not knowing whether the music or the words
frustrated us more, we waited in fearful silence for what
had to come next. And for the last time the expressionless
voice spoke:

Two weeks later, when a road-crew dug out the car,
they found inside it the frozen corpse of a young woman,
incredibly tranquil and serene. Between the blue and rigid
lips was the pencil-thin column of ash from a hand-rolled
cigarette, which had burned undisturbed until it had
seared the lips and gone out. The crew-boss silenced his
men, radioed a call to the State Police with remarkable
calm . . .
And then went home and made savage love to his wife.

And that damned unnerving guitar fell to pieces on the E
minor sixth, as resolved as it was ever going to be.

The silence persisted for a full minute before anyone so
much as thought to look into his drink for any answers that
might be skulking around in there. And when we did, we
found none there, so we tried looking at each other. And

when that failed, we turned as one to regard the stranger who had brought us this vision. His hand was back at his side, now, and the fireplace was back where it belonged, naively attempting to warm a room that had gone as cold as death . . .

"That, gentlemen," he said simply, "is Bobbi Joy."

No one said a word. I saw Doc Webster groping desperately for a wisecrack to break the spell, and it just wasn't there. The stranger had been right: now that it was over we could scarcely believe that it had happened, scarcely believe that we were still alive.

"Now that you know her," the stranger went on, "you're ready to hear her story, what made her what she is and what I hope to do about it."

Bobbi Joy (the Meddler continued) was born Isadora Brickhill in the back seat of a gypsy cab somewhere in Harlem, in the year 1952. I can see by your scowls, gentlemen, that I don't have to explain what *that* means. She didn't even have Billie Holiday's classic two choices—no one was hiring maids in those days. By the training and education she received, she was prepared only for the most basic trade there is: by 1966 little Isadora was an experienced and, if rumor is to be believed, accomplished whore.

Even in that most clichéd of professions she was an anomaly. She did not drink, touched no drugs save an occasional social reefer, and never seemed to project that desperate air of defeat and cynical surrender so characteristic of her colleagues. She had a fiery fighting spirit that demanded and elicited respect from all who knew her, and except for physically, no one ever touched her at all. Madams loved her for her utterly dependable honesty in the split, the girls loved her for her unflagging courage and willingness to be of help, and the johns loved her for the completely detached professionalism she brought to her work.

Then came the bust.

Some sort of political mix-up, as the story goes—a payoff missed, an official inadvertently offended, a particularly well-written expose that demanded token action. Whatever the reason, Hannah's House was raided in April of 1974 in the traditional manner, wagons and all. Bobbi, as she was by now known, was loaded into the wagons with the rest of the girls before she had a chance to grab a wrap. Consequently she attracted the attention of a patrolman named Duffy, who had come to appreciate that in such situations, a policeman hath rank privileges. He attempted to collect what he regarded as only his right, and was refused: Bobbi allowed as how she might be for sale but she was damned if she was for free. Duffy persisted, and bought a knee in the groin, whereupon he lost all discretion and laid open Bobbi's face with the barrel of his pistol. This so mightily embarrassed Duffy's sergeant, who was also Duffy's brother-in-law, that he was forced to ignore the wound, locking Bobbi in with the rest of the girls in the hope that her disfigurement could be passed off as the result of a razor fight in the cells. By the time she got medical attention, it was too late. She was scarred through and through, and forever unsuited for the only job she knew.

Almost a year later, a producer received an unsolicited tape in the mail. Such tapes are *never* played, but this one had the songs listed on the outside, and the producer's eye was caught by the first title: "The Suicide Song." It was a crude, home-taped version of the song you just heard, audio only. The producer played it once, and spent a frantic seventeen hours locating Bobbi Joy.

He didn't make her a star: he simply recorded her songs and made them available for sale. She *became* a star, a star like there had never been before. At least seven of her recordings, tape and holo, were proscribed from public broadcast—because areas in which they were played showed sudden jumps in the suicide rate. The 70's and 80's were not good years in which to live, and Bobbi Joy spoke for all too many of us all too well. She was a phenomenon, endlessly analyzed and never defined, and if some of us took a perverse kind of courage from her songs, maybe that was more reflection of us than of her. And maybe not.

In any event, the producer with remarkable ease became unspeakably rich. And it comforted him not. Poor devil, condemned to be the man who gave Bobbi Joy to the world, how could his heart be soothed with money? He gave most of it away to his mad brother, who thought he could build a time-machine, just to be rid of it. He pickled himself in alcohol with the balance, and never, ever played her tapes for himself. Like all her fans, he ached to bring her peace and knew no man ever could; but there was more. He loved her with a ferocious and utterly hopeless desperation, and consequently avoided her company as much as possible. He dreamed futile dreams of fixing her hurt, and lost a great deal of weight, and when his mad brother told him one spring day that the time machine was a success, he knew what he had to do.

His brother, though mad, was not so mad as he was by now, and sought to reason with him. He spoke of possible disruption of the time-stream by the changing of the past, and other complicated things, and flatly forbade the producer to use the time-machine.

Right now, years in the future, he's nursing a sore jaw and wondering whether I'm about to destroy the fabric of time. And so am I.

I've been wandering around in your time for two or three days. I gave myself some leeway to make plans, but I've been using it to cool off. And now I don't know what to do. Maybe my brother was right; he knows a lot more than I about it. *But I can't leave her in pain, can I?*

Oh yes, one more thing: the bust is tonight. About four hours from now.

What could we say? We had to believe him—the technology inherent in that holographic sphere was certainly well beyond the present state of the art. More important, if that voice truly existed in our time, we would have heard of it long since. It was impossible to disbelieve that voice.

Callahan summed it up for all of us.

"What do you figure to do about it, brother?"

The Meddler didn't answer, and suddenly I knew somehow, maybe from the set of his mouth, maybe a little from the glance he gave Tommy Janssen.

"I think I understand, Mike," I said softly. "I saw him talking to Tommy while I was up on the stand, and I saw Tommy cuss him out. Somewhere outside he ran into someone who told him where he could find a kid who used to be a heroin addict, a kid who would certainly know where to get him a gun. He's going to kill Patrolman Duffy. Aren't you, friend?"

The Meddler nodded.

"Then you've made your decision?" asked Callahan. "One murder'll fix everything?"

"It'll prevent that scar," said the Meddler. "And how can it be murder to kill a scum like that? The hell with a gun, I can get within knife distance easily—no one will be expecting anything, and I don't care what they do to me afterwards." He squared his shoulders, and looked Callahan in the eye. "You figure to stop me?"

"Well now, son," Callahan drawled, "I'm not certain I've got the right to meddle in something like this. Besides, I reckon it's no accident you're closer to the door than any of us. But it seems like I ought to point out—"

He broke off and stared at the doorway. So did the rest

of us. A man stood there, where there had been no one a moment before. He looked like an older, wearier version of the Meddler, built much the same, but he wasn't wearing an overcoat so you could see that the pot-belly was actually an enormous belt strapped around his waist. Obviously, it was a time-machine; just as obviously, he was its inventor, come to stop his brother from tampering with history.

But our attention was centered not on the machinery around his waist, but on the much smaller piece of it in his right hand. Made of glass and seemingly quite fragile, it could only have been the handgun of the 1990's, and the way he held it told us that we ought to respect it. I thought of lasers and backed away, fetching up against my amplifier.

"I can't let you do it, John," said the newcomer, ignoring the rest of us.

"You can't stop me," said the Meddler.

"I can kill you," his brother corrected.

"Look, Henry," the Meddler said desperately, "I'm not going into this blindly. I know what I'm doing."

"Do you?" His brother laughed. "You damned fool, you haven't the faintest notion what you could do by killing that fool policeman. Suppose a criminal he would have apprehended goes on to kill some innocent people instead? Suppose the simple removal of him from history suffices to disrupt this time-stream beyond repair? You may be killing every man, woman and child in your time, John!"

"Don't you think I know that?" cried the man in the overcoat. "And do you suppose that's all there is to be afraid of? Suppose I'm entirely successful, and only bring about a world without Bobbi Joy. She brought us all a self-conscious awareness of collective guilt which had an enormous effect for good. *I don't know that I have the right to deprive the world of her music.*

"Suppose there's a Law of Conservation of Pain? Suppose pain can't be destroyed within a continuum? Then all I'll have done is redirected her pain: I suspect it will all be transferred to *me*—and I can't sing worth a damn. Henry, I admit I don't have any idea what the consequences of my action may be. But I do know what I have to do."

"And I can't let you," his brother repeated.

He lifted the strange glass pistol and aimed it at the Meddler's heart, and I saw Callahan's big hands go under the bar for the sawed-off shotgun, and I saw Long-Drink and the Doc and Tommy Janssen start to close in on the gunman, and I knew that none of them would be in time, and without thinking I spun on my heel, twisted the volume knob savagely on my amp, clutched my E-string as high as I could and snapped the pick across it. A shrieking high-note lanced through the air, and I rammed the guitar in front of the monitor-speaker for maximum feedback.

A red-hot knife went through every ear in the room, freezing the action like a stop-motion camera. The guitar fed back and fed back, building from a noise like a gutshot pig to something that was felt rather than heard. Glasses began to shatter along the bar, then bottles on the long shelves behind it . . .

And all at once, so did that deadly little glass gun.

Quickly I muted the guitar, and our ears rang for a lingering minute. Blood ran from a couple of cuts on Callahan's face, and the gunman's hand was a mess. Doc Webster was at his side somehow, producing bandages and antiseptic from his everpresent black bag and steering the wounded man into a seat.

The Meddler sat down beside him. "How did you do it, Henry? I thought I had the only—"

"You do," Henry snapped. "You came back with it, you bloody maniac, and as soon as you reappeared I knew from the look on your face that you had succeeded. I didn't wait around to find out what change you'd made in the world I knew; I hit you with a chair and took the belt, determined to make one last desperate try to save my time. You laughed as you went down, and now I guess I know why. *Meddler!*"

The Meddler stood up, faced Callahan. "You've got a gun under that bar," he stated. "I want it."

Callahan stood his ground. "Not a chance," he said.

"Then I'll knife him, or bash in his skull with a rock, or drop a match in his gas-tank." He headed for the door, and no one got in his way.

"Hold on a minute," I called out, and he stopped.

"Look," he told me, "I'm grateful for what you did, but—"

"Listen," I interrupted, "maybe we can't give you a gun . . . but we can sure pass the hat for you."

His jaw dropped as I whipped off the eleven-gallon hat and offered it to Noah Gonzalez. Noah dropped in a five-dollar bill without hesitating, and passed the hat to Slippery Joe. People began digging into their pockets, emptying their wallets, and dropping the swag in the hat as it came their way. It filled rapidly, and by the time it reached Fast Eddie I guess it had maybe a hundred dollars or better in it.

Eddie took it from Callahan and looked at the Meddler. "I ain't got no dough," he announced, "but I got a '65 Chevy outside dat'll do a hunnert'n'ten easy." He fished out a set of keys and dropped them into the hat. "Don't waste no time parkin' the bastard, you'll never find a parkin' space in Harlem dis time o' night. Double park it; I'll pick it up from de cops tomorra."

There were tears running down the Meddler's face; he seemed unable to speak.

"Okay," said Callahan briskly, "you've got three or four hours. That should be plenty of time. You drive to

Hannah's as fast as you can, wave around that dough and tell Hannah you want to take one of the girls home for the night. She sees all that cabbage, she'll go for it. That'll get Bobbi clear of the bust, and what happens after that is up to you. Good luck.''

He took the hat from Eddie and handed it to the Meddler, who took it with a trembling hand.

"Th-thank you," the Meddler said. "I . . . I hope I'm doing the right thing."

"You're doing what you have to do," said Callahan, "and you don't have to kill anyone. Now get out of here."

The Meddler got.

We sent his brother home eventually, and Eddie and I packed up our equipment for the night. We felt sort of inadequate after having heard Bobbi Joy, and anyway everyone in the joint was broke now. By closing time, we were all ready to leave.

The next night we were all there by seven, and although it was Punday Night nobody felt much like making jokes. A few of us had tried to get news of the previous night's raid from the police, but they weren't talking, and we were as filled with suspense as the fireplace was with glass.

Along about eight the sporadic conversation was silenced by the sudden appearance of the time-traveling belt on the bar, a soft green sphere and a single piece of paper encircled in it. The piece of paper proved to be a note, which read:

Didn't want to leave you hanging. Please destroy this belt. The next time we all might not be so lucky. Many thanks from both of us.

Callahan tossed the belt into the fireplace, and it landed with a crunching sound. Then he picked up the sphere, and held it in his big hand. For the second time in two days, the fireplace faded from sight, but this time it was replaced by a mountain stream, crisp clean pines in the background, an achingly beautiful sunset playing tag with ominous grey stormclouds.

Bobbi Joy sat by the stream, her guitar across her lap, and her unscarred face was more beautiful than all the sunsets that ever were. She gazed serenely at all of us, and fitted her fingers to the strings.

It began slowly, a simple statement of key woven out of ninth chords that rose and fell like cyclical hopes in a crazy time-signature. Gradually, the pauses between the ringing chords were filled in with rhythmic direction, picking up speed and becoming almost a calypso beat—save that calypso never used such chords. And Bobbi Joy sang:

> *I walk around with . . . doubt inside of me*
> *I don't believe in . . . what I try to be*
> *Words I whisper . . . seem like a lie to me*
> *Strange thing*
> *Wonder what's happening?*

Her voice spoke of confusion and fear, of doubt and loneliness; and our hearts sank within us.

> *I'm scared that maybe . . . I'm what I seem to be*
> *Today is only . . . another dream to me*
> *Fading quickly . . . from my memory*
> *Strange thing*
> *Wonder what's happening?*

All around the room I saw men respond to that plaintive question, saw them wince at the thought of failure, as Bobbi Joy went into the bridge of her song. Cradled in strings and an ironically mellow organ, she went on:

> *The sky is changing color*
> *And the ground is far away*
> *I wandered in my mind*
> *And now I've lost the way . . .*

Where are the places . . . that I used to go?
Who are the people . . . that I used to know?
Will things be any . . . better tomorrow?
Strange thing
Wonder what's happening?

And then, cutting through our despair as the sun cut through the holographic clouds, a full orchestra came out of nowhere, a warm carpet of sound that swelled in moments to an almost Wagnerian peak. Bobbi's face was transfused with a startling smile of pure joy, and full-throated she sang:

And then I meet a Meddler
And the Meddler comes to me
He tells me of my future
And he comforts me . . .

And the final verse exploded in Callahan's Place like a hallelujah chorus of horns and violins, banishing all the fear and the uncertainty and the pain, turning them all to nothing more than paid dues, the admission price to happiness:

Now rain is falling . . . like a beautitude
Trees are weeping . . . tears of gratitude
There's been a change in . . . my whole attitude
Strange thing
Good things are happening
Strange thing—
Good things are happening

And with a flurry of trumpets, the song died. Bobbi Joy smiled a deep, satisfied smile and disappeared, taking her mountain stream with her.

Callahan's arm came down fast, and the sphere exploded in the center of the fireplace. And in that moment we realized, all of us in Callahan's Place, that the Meddler's guess had been part right. Just as there are laws of Conservation of Matter and Energy, so there are in fact Laws of Conservation of Pain and Joy. Neither can ever be created or destroyed.

But one can be converted into the other.

6

Just Dessert

Sooner or later, just about every bar acquires that most obnoxious of nuisances: the practical joker. I'd have thought Callahan's Place would be immune to that particular kind of carbuncle—we don't seem to pick up the standard idiots that most saloons have to put up with, the weepy drunks and the belligerent loudmouths and the ones who drink to get stupider. It's almost as though some sort of protective spell ensures that the only people who find Callahan's are the ones who should—and the ones who must.

But very occasionally, some refugee from the Dew Drop Inn does accidentally wander in, usually for just long enough to make us appreciate his absence when he finally leaves. There was, for instance, the guy of an ethnic extraction I can't specify without getting a lot of Italians mad at me, who represented a juke-box concern. He made Callahan an offer he couldn't refuse—so Mike didn't bother refusing. The guy's broken arms eventually healed, I understand, but he never got over the amnesia. Then there was the gent who brought his young secretary in to get her drunk for carnal purposes. Callahan got a little sloppy that night: somehow all the ginger ale ended up in her glass and all the vodka in his. When he woke up he was a far piece from nowhere, minus a secretary and a rather sporty pair of pants.

When the Practical Joker arrived, however, it was not Callahan but Doc Webster who fixed his wagon.

It was a Friday night, and the place was more crowded than Dollar Day in a cathouse. Fast Eddie was sharing his piano bench with three other guys, Callahan and Tom Hauptman were behind the bar, busier than a midget mountain-climber, and we were plumb out of beer nuts. Me, I was sandwiched between Doc Webster and Noah Gonzalez at the bar, feeling the urgency of hydraulic pressure, wishing there wasn't a wall of folks between me and the jake.

I guess it was the huge number of cars scattered around out in the parking lot that made that sadistic jackass think he'd found the perfect place to pull off his little gag. Come to think on it, maybe Fate was leading him to Callahan's after all.

In any case, he came shouldering through the throng with his two buddies on either side of him at about eleven, and the three of them took up position at the bar just beside the Doc. I noticed them out of the corner of my eye and gaped like a fish with lockjaw. The guy in the middle was plainly and simply the ugliest man I had ever seen.

When they passed out necks he thought they said "sex" and asked for lots and lots. His chin and his Adam's apple looked like twin brothers in bunk beds, his nose appeared to be on sideways, and his eyes were different sizes. His ears were so prominent that from the front he looked like a taxicab coming down the street with the doors open, and his hair resembled a lawn with persistent crabgrass. The longest strands issued from his nostrils. As he reached the bar, the clock over the cashbox stopped, and I couldn't blame it a bit. I forgot about my bladder and gulped the drink I'd been nursing.

The Doc saw my face, swiveled his massive bulk around to look, and damn' near dropped his Scotch; you have to understand that the Doc firmly believes in the Irish legend that on Judgement Day you will be suspended head-down in a barrel containing all the liquor you've ever spilled, and if you drown, to Hell with you. Even Callahan shuddered.

The guy glanced at the perfectly ordinary-looking accomplices on either side of him, pulled a fistful of singles from the pocket of his sportscoat, and said, "Boilermakers." The noise of the crowd had begun to abate as folks caught sight of the apparition, and the single word was plainly audible.

Callahan's cigar traveled from one side of his mouth to the other. He shrugged his broad shoulders and produced three shotglasses and three chasers, unable to take his eyes off the guy in the middle.

The three of them lifted their shots, upended them, then did the same with the beers.

"Again," said the ugly man, and Callahan refilled their glasses.

The second round went down, if anything, faster than the first.

"Again."

Callahan blinked, shrugged again and made three more boilers.

Gulp-gulp-gulp.

Now, even in Callahan's Place on a Friday night, amid some of the most dedicated drinkers that ever tried to outdo a sponge, this sort of thing is bound to attract some attention. The silence was nearly complete; some of the boys in the far corners began climbing up on tables and chairs to watch, and there were enough necks being craned to make a chiropractor dizzy with glee. Over at the piano Fast Eddie began a pool, taking bets on how many more rounds the three strangers could survive.

After the sixth set of boilers had been made and unmade, Callahan tried to call a halt. "Sorry, gents. If you want to commit suicide, you'll have to find another joint."

The two flankers nodded, but the ugly man reached into his sports coat pocket again, produced a chopstick, and balanced it on his index finger. "Peter Piper picked a peck of pickled peppers," he said clearly and distinctly. "British constitution. The Leith police dismisseth us. Sister Suzie's sewing shirts for soldiers . . ."

He kept it up until Callahan, exchanging looks with Doc Webster, put another shot in front of him. The guy shut up and gulped the sauce, sent a glass of beer after it, and waited expectantly.

Callahan sighed and opened a fresh bottle, and I could tell from the label that it was the colored water Tom Hauptman drinks when he's working (explaining to anyone who'll listen that "The wages of gin are breath"). I guess the big barkeep figured this mug was too far gone to notice the difference.

But as he reached out to pour, the unlovely customer put his hand over his glass. "Wait a bit," he said faintly, his voice suddenly wavering. "I . . . I don't know. Maybe I . . . oh Lord, I don't feel too good. I think I'm gonna be . . ." He clutched his middle and leaned over the bar, and a ghastly mess splattered on the counter-top.

A great disgusted groan went up, and those of the boys with weak stomachs began to make their way toward the door.

But the *real* stampede began when the hapless stranger's two companions, grinning wildly, produced a pair of spoons and dug in.

I would have bet my store teeth that nothing short of an earthquake could empty Callahan's Place on a Friday night, but that about did it. Folks fled in all directions, out the front door, the back door, even the *windows*, horror on every face, hideous gargling cries fading into the night.

When the smoke had cleared and the commotion ceased, Callahan, the Doc and I were the only survivors, and even the indomitable Callahan looked green about the gills. Tom was out cold on the floor behind the bar.

And that damned practical joker and his two cronies turned around, looked at the empty saloon, and began laughing hard enough to bust a gut, slapping their thighs and punching each other on the shoulder.

"What the *hell* . . ." I began, and the ugly man, looking fully recovered now, turned to face me, still laughing fit to kill. He pulled open his sports coat, disclosing a hot water bottle pinned over the inside pocket. "Beef stew," he gasped, and his pals began laughing even harder.

Callahan went from pale green to bright red, and his hand went under the bar, emerging with a softball bat.

"No, Mike!" I cried, "Don't! I know how you feel, but there's just a wild chance that some jury somewhere in the world might convict you."

Muscles bulged in his jaw, but he got a grip on himself and lowered the bat. The three waterheads kept on chortling, oblivious.

"All RIGHT, goddammit," Callahan bellowed. "You've had yer fun. Now get the rest o' this crap off my bar and get outa here before I murder yez." I was startled to notice that Doc was grinning broadly. It didn't figure to be his kind of humor.

The three wits, sensing danger at last, nodded and began spooning up the remains of the stew. In no time the bar-top was reasonably clean. The ugly joker offered Callahan a ten-spot for his trouble, and nearly had it for dessert. Still smiling idiotically, they headed for the door and disappeared into the night.

Callahan caught sight of the Doc's grin and glared at him, still furious. "What the hell are *you* laughin' at?" he growled, and the Doc's grin got even wider.

"I saw that gag pulled once before, Mike," he said, "and I recognized it right off."

"So that makes it funny?"

"Hell, no."

"Well then?"

"That guy's stomach must be pretty good to handle all that booze," the Doc said happily, "but I wonder how he and his buddies are gonna like the seasoning I put in the stew while their backs were turned."

The Doc opened his pudgy fist, and there was a little bottle in it, labeled, "serum of ipecac."

Callahan's eyes widened, and then he smiled.

7

"A Voice Is Heard In Ramah . . ."

How should I know?

It was a combination of things, I guess, and no one special reason. For one thing, the place doesn't look like much from the outside. Nor is the interior by any stretch of the imagination romantic—more like a cross between a Chinese firedrill and Tim Finnegan's last party, most nights. But then you can't tell that from the highway either. Whatever the reason, it just sort of turned out that women didn't come into Callahan's Place.

All right, maybe I'm ducking the issue. Maybe there was some kind of masculine aura about the place, a psychic emanation of chauvinist-piggery that kept it a male bastion for so long. Maybe we were extended adolescents, emotionally retarded, projecting a telepathic equivalent of the "No Girls Allowed" sign on Tubby's clubhouse. There's surely no doubt that Callahan's is culturally descended from the grand tradition of Irish bars, and they tend to be misogynistic. Long-Drink McGonnigle's father-in-law, Thirsty O'Toole, assures us that Irishmen go to pubs to get shut of the women.

But I can't really believe there was ever any prejudice intended. Callahan doesn't insist that his customers be *human*. Certainly no effort was ever made to bar women, as happened at McSorley's. But men didn't come to Callahan's Place to meet women, and that may be why the few that chanced to drop in generally left quickly.

Then one night a woman walked in and stayed, and I was real proud of the way the boys acted.

It was a Punday Night, as it happened, a little late in the evening. A perfectly good topic—"trees"—had been worked over for so long that the three surviving contestants, Doc Webster, Tom Flannery, and Long-Drink, were . . . pardon me . . . stumped. Callahan declared all three co-winners and, as custom demanded, refunded their might's tab. But as it was still a bit early we decided to hold a play-off for Grand Pundit, no holds barred, any topic, and the three champions agreed.

Long-Drink led off, his eyes filled with that terrible gleam that presages a true stinker. They call him Long-Drink because he is one long drink of water: when he sits he looks like he's standing, and when he stands he looks like three other guys. He doesn't mass much more than a pickup truck, and he is the only man I know who can talk and drink whiskey at the same time. He does a lot of both.

"Gentlemen," he drawled, demonstrating the trick, "the story I am about to relate takes place in the distant future. Interstellar travel is commonplace; contacts with alien races are familiar experiences. One day, however, a planet is discovered out Antares way whose sole inhabitant is an enormous humanoid, three miles high and made of granite. At first it is mistaken for an immense statue left by some vanished race of giants, for it squats motionless on a yellow plain, exhibiting no outward sign of life. It has legs, but it never rises to walk on them. It has a mouth, but never eats or speaks. It has what appears to be a perfectly functional brain, the size of a four-story condominium, but the organ lies dormant, electrochemical activity at a standstill. Yet it lives.

"This puzzles the hell out of the scientists, who try everything they can think of to get some sign of life from the behemoth—in vain. It just squats, motionless and seemingly thoughtless, until one day a xenobiologist, frustrated beyond endurance, screams, 'How could evolution give legs, mouth and brain to a creature that doesn't use them?'

"It happens that he's the first one to ask a direct question in the thing's presence. It rises with a thunderous rumble to its full height, scattering the clouds, thinks for a second, booms, 'IT COULDN'T,' and squats down again.

" 'Migod,' exclaims the xenobiologist, 'Of course! *It only stands to reason.*' "

There was an extended pause, in which the sound of Long-Drink blinking was plainly audible. Then a hailstorm of glasses, full and empty, burst in the fireplace, loud enough to drown out the great collective groan. Doc Webster's eyes rolled briefly, like loaded dice, and came up snake eyes. Callahan began passing our fresh drinks with a slightly stunned expression.

The Doc contemplated a while, looking a lot like some

of the merrier representations of the Buddha. "Bug-eyed punster sort of stuff, eh? Say, did you boys ever hear of the planet where the inhabitants were mobile flowers? Remarkably similar to Earthly blossoms, but they had feet and humanlike intelligence. The whole planet, from the biggest bouquet to the smallest corsage, was ruled over by a king named Richard the Artichoke Heart . . . anyhow, one day a pale-eyed perennial caught Richard's eye at a court orgy, and . . ."

I tuned the Doc out for a second. Fast Eddie, sensing some truly legendary horror in the offing, had stealthily left his piano stool and began edging casually toward the fire extinguisher in the corner, an expression of rapt attention on his monkey face. There's enough of the Doc to make two or three good targets, but I sidled out of the line of fire all the same.

". . . the smitten monarch engaged royal tutors of all sorts, to no avail," the Doc was saying. "Artists, musicians, philosophers, scientists and mathematicians failed alike to engage the attention of the witless concubine, whose only apparent interest was in gathering pollen. At last the embarrassed Richard gave her up as hopeless and had some Rotenone slipped into her soup. As he exclaimed to this prime minister later that night, 'I can lead a horticulture but I can't make her think!' " The Doc's poker face was perfect.

And in the terrible pause that ensued, before Eddie could trigger the extinguisher, a clear, sweet, contralto voice asked, "What sort of flower was she?" and every head in the place swung toward the door like weathervanes in a windstorm.

And there she was.

She was a big woman, but none of it was extra, and she stood framed in the doorway with an easy grace that a ballerina might have envied. Her hair was long and straight, the color of polished obsidian. Her skin was fair without being pale, and she wore a long-sleeved, high-necked dress of royal purple that brushed sawdust from the floor. She was pretty enough to make a preacher kick a hole in a stained-glass window.

She fielded the combined stares of a couple dozen goggle-eyed males with no effort at all, a half-smile playing at the corners of her mouth, and I had the distinct feeling that we could all have turned into three-headed tree frogs without disturbing her composure in the least. Perhaps that was why our own composure was so manifestly smithereened and scattered to the four winds—but I'm more inclined to think it was the one-two sledgehammer punch of, *A woman in Callahan's?* followed by the equally startling, *Why the hell not?* What shocked us the most was that we had no idea why we should be so shocked. Like opening a ginger ale and finding Jamesons' inside: nothing wrong with it, but it sort of takes you by surprise.

Doc Webster tried unsuccessfully to clear his throat; his poker face was now royally flushed. "I . . . uh," he stammered, "don't know *what* kind of . . . uh . . . flower she was, young lady."

A grin stuck red lips back from perfect teeth. "I just thought," she said clearly, "that the king might be suffering from fuchsia shock."

There was a pause, and the soft, subtle sound of eyeballs glazing: you can only absorb so much at once. But Callahan rose magnificently to the occasion.

"Sure and begonia," he breathed.

"Oh," she gasped, and blinked. "Perhaps I shouldn't be here. I didn't realize this was an Iris bar."

Long-Drink choked, spraying Bushmill's like a six-foot-seven aerosol. And suddenly we were all roaring, hooting, rocking with laughter, the kind that leaves your eyes wet and your sides sore. The timbers rang with merriment, a happy release of tension.

"Lord, lord," the Doc gasped, wiping his eyes and clutching at his ample belly, "nobody's made a straight man out of me in twenty years. Whoooo-ee!" He shook his head ruefully, still chuckling.

"Lady," said Callahan, a world of meaning in the words, "you'll do." There was respect in his whiskey baritone, and a strange, deep satisfaction. She acknowledged the former with a nod and stepped into the room.

The bar had been crowded, but by the time she reached it she had enough room to park a truck, and a wide choice of seats. She picked one and sat gracefully, making a small noise of surprise and delight. "I never thought I'd see an armchair this tall," she said to Callahan, setting her purse on the bar.

"I don't believe in bar stools," Callahan explained. "A man should be comfortable when he drinks."

"A man?" she asked pointedly.

"Oh, a woman ought to be comfortable all the time," he agreed solemnly. "Hey, Eddie?"

"Yeah, boss?"

"You want to open a window? I think I smell bra smoke."

She reddened.

I looked at Eddie, was surprised to see a glare instead of a grin. *Migod,* I thought crazily. *Fast Eddie has been smit.* It didn't seem possible; ever since his wife divorced him a few years back, Eddie had been a confirmed loner.

"Touché," she conceded at last. "I had no call to criticize your speech patterns. I'm sorry."

"No problem," Callahan assured her. "My name's Mike." He stuck out a big calloused hand.

She shook it gravely. "I am Rachel."

"What'll it be, Rachel?"

"Bourbon, please."

Callahan nodded, turned around and began mixing I. W. Harper and ice cubes in the proper proportions. She opened her purse, removed a wallet from it and pulled out a five-dollar bill, and I found that I was talking.

"I'm afraid you can't use that fin in here, Rachel." It felt strange not to be paralyzed.

She turned to me, and I saw her eyes for the first time close up, and I felt my tongue being retied tighter than ever. I don't know how to describe those eyes except to say that they looked impossibly *old*, older than eyes could be. There was some pain in them, sure—most people that Fate leads to Callahan's Place have anguished eyes when they first arrive—but beyond the pain was a kind of unspeakable weariness, a terrible and ancient knowledge that had not brought satisfaction. My memory churned, and produced the only remotely similar pair of eyes I have ever seen: my grandmother, dead of cancer these twenty years.

"I beg your pardon?" she said politely, and I tried hard to climb back up out of her eyes. Tom Flannery sensed my distress and came to my aid.

"Jake's right, Rachel," he said. "Callahan doesn't believe in cash registers either. He only deals in singles."

"You mean everything in the house costs a dollar?" she asked in surprise.

"Oh, no," Tom demurred. "Everything in the house costs fifty cents. There's a cigar box full of quarters down there—see?—and you pick up your change on the way out . . . *if* you've left your glass on the bar."

"What's the alternative?" she asked with a puzzled frown, as Callahan set her drink down before her.

"Smash your glass in the fireplace," Callahan said cheerfully. "Does you a world of good sometimes. It's worth fifty cents, easy."

Her whole face brightened. "A long time ago," she

said thoughtfully, "I bought an entire house for the single purpose of smashing crockery in it. I think I like your place, Mike."

"That makes two of us," he said comfortably, and poured himself a beer mug of Bushmill's best.

"To Callahan's Place," she said, draining her glass in one easy motion and holding it high. Callahan didn't bat an eye. He inhaled his own whiskey as fast as it'd pour and raised his glass too. Two arms fell as one.

Glass shattered in the fireplace, and a spontaneous cheer went up from all around. Long-Drink McGonnigle began singing, "For She's a Jolly Good Fellow," and was stifled without ceremony.

She turned to face us. "Lots of bars make a woman feel welcome," she said. "This is the first one that ever made me feel *at home*. Thank you all."

Ever see a whole bar blush?

Fast Eddie came in the door—no one had seen him leave—with change of a five from the all-night deli across the street and gave it to her gravely, a solemn look on his wrinkled face. But Callahan refused the single she offered. One exquisite eyebrow rose quizzically.

"Rachel," he said, "this here is Punday Night at my Place, and the champeen punster doesn't have to pay his . . . or her . . . bar bill. From what I've heard already, I'd say you've got a shot at the title." Her face lit with a merry smile. Callahan explained the format and the subject we were using and built her another drink.

She paused a moment in thought. "The Middle East," she began at last, "finally achieved a kind of uneasy stability in the late 1970's. Israel and the Pan-Arabian nations maintaining a fragile truce. Then one day the Arabian ambassador to Israel, Opinh Bom Bey, chanced to spy a carousel in the market place and, being intrigued by this Westernish recreation, decided to try it. Being a neophyte, he became extremely dizzy, dismounted from his wooden steed with great difficulty, and reeled out of the square. A Chinese shepherd called Ewe Hu was passing through Jerusalem at that time with three fine sheep, and Bom Bey staggered into their midst. The middle sheep promptly ate him.

"Horrific visions of the war that would inevitably ensue racing through his mind, Ewe Hu flung up his hands and cried, 'Middle lamb, you've had a dizzy Bey!' "

There was a ghastly silence, such as must exist on the airless wastes of the Moon, and Callahan's ever-present cigar fell from his lips, landing with an absurdly loud splash in his glass. Oblivious, he lifted the glass and drank. When he set it down again, the cigar was back in his teeth, soggy and drooping.

Long-Drink made a face. "You didn't keep to the subject," he complained feebly, and Fast Eddie began to cloud up.

But she stood her ground, deadpan. "The story," she maintained, "was clearly about Zion's friction."

And the silence fell in a million shards, whoops of laughter, blending in with groans and the volley of breaking glass on the hearth.

Tom Flannery entered a forfeit about the same time Long-Drink and the Doc conceded defeat, and that was Rachel's first night at Callahan's Place. She returned on the following night, and then on the following Tuesday, and soon became something of a regular. She was there when Tommy Janssen got married right in front of the fireplace, and the night the Place caught fire, and that sad night when gentle, softly smiling Tom Flannery finally failed to show up (Tom's doctors had given him nine months to live, the day before he happened into Callahan's Place), and she just seemed to fit. Although she was never by any stretch of the imagination One Of The Boys, she fit in a way that reminded me very faintly of Wendy in

Never-Never Land. But she was not disturbed by the hooliganry of her Lost Boys, nor dismayed by their occasional ribaldry—once when Doc Webster, slightly jealous of her superior puns, tried to embarrass her with an off-color joke, she responded with a gag so steamy and so hilarious that the Doc blushed clear down to his ankles and laughed himself silly. And she was incredibly gentle with Fast Eddie, who came to display the classic signs of a man goofy with love. Suddenly all he knew how to play was torch songs, and while she always praised them, she pointedly missed the point, yet somehow allowed him to keep his self-respect.

Curiously, Eddie was the only one of us to fall for her. Certainly, all of us at Callahan's were heir to the tradition of the B-movie—and the A-movie for that matter—that any female who enters your life in a dramatic manner must be your fated love. But somehow Rachel didn't elicit that reflex of imagined desire in us. She was never cold—you retained at all times an impression of vibrant feminity—but she never projected either the air of receptivity which provokes passes, or the studied indifference which is the same thing in disguise. We never even learned much about her, where she lived and that sort of thing. All we knew was that she was fun to be with: she was a note of nearly pure cheer even in a place where good cheer was commonplace.

But only nearly pure. There were those eyes. They reminded me in many ways of Mickey Finn's eyes when he first came around, and I knew it was only a matter of time before the right toast would unlock her heart and let out all that pain. Hell, we all knew it—but she had to do it herself. You don't pry in Callahan's Place.

It was nearly four months before she finally opened up, a Thursday I believe it was. She'd been abstracted lately, still taking part in convivial banter but strangely distant too, and I was half-expecting what happened.

Doc Webster had come bustling in about nine, later than usual for him on a Thursday since he has no hospital duties that night. So he bought a round for the house and explained. If asked, the Doc will assist at home birthings, a practice he's been at some pains to keep from the attention of both the AMA and the Suffolk County Police Department ever since the great Midwife Busts at the Santa Cruz Birth Center a few years back. Doc says that pregnant women aren't sick, that a lady ought to call the tune at her own birthing, all other things being equal—he has oxygen and other useful things in his car, and he hasn't lost one yet.

"She was a primipara," he said with satisfaction, "but her pelvic clearance was adequate, presentation was classic, she did a modified Lamaze, and damned well too. Fine healthy boy, eight pounds and some, sucking like a bilge pump the last I saw him. Lord, I'm thirsty myself."

Somehow news of new life makes you feel just plain good, and the Doc's own joy was contagious. When the last glass had been filled, we all stood up and faced the fireplace. "TO MOTHERHOOD!" we bellowed together, and it rained glasses for a while.

And when the racket had stopped, we heard a sound from inside the joint's single rest room, a literally unmistakable sound.

Rachel. Weeping.

Absurd situation. Over two dozen alarmed and anxious men, accustomed to dropping everything and running to anyone in pain. All of us clustered around the bathroom door (labeled "Folks") like winos outside a soup kitchen, and not one of us with the guts to open up the damned door because *there's a lady in there*. Fast Eddie's ferocious glare would have stopped us if scruples hadn't. Confused and mortally embarrassed, we shuffled our feet and looked for something tactful to say. Inside, the sobbing persisted, muted now.

Callahan coughed. "Rachel?"

She broke off crying. "Y . . . yes?"

"You gonna be long? My back teeth are floatin'."

Pause.

"Not long, Mike. I'll hurry."

"Take your time," he rumbled.

She did, but eventually the door opened and she came out, no tear tracks evident, obviously in control again. Callahan mumbled thanks, glared around at us furiously and went in.

We came to our senses and began bustling aimlessly around the room, looking at anything but Rachel, talking spiritedly. Callahan flushed it almost at once and came back out, looking as innocent as a face like that will let him. He went back behind the bar, dusting his meaty hands.

Rachel was sitting at the bar, staring at where a mirror would be if Callahan believed in encouraging narcissism: plain bare wall criss-crossed with all the epigrams, proverbs and puns Callahan's found worth recording over the past I-don't-know-how many years of . . . ahem . . . flashing wit. The one she was looking at was attributed to a guy named Robinson. It said: "A man should live forever or die trying."

"Women too, I suppose?" she asked it.

Callahan looked puzzled, and she pointed to the quote. He studied it a minute, then turned back to her.

"You got a better idea?"

She shrugged, held out her hand. The big barkeep filled it with a glass of I. W. Harper and poured one for himself. The sparkling conversation going on around the room seemed to sort of run down. She sipped daintily . . . then said a word I'd never heard her use before and gulped the rest.

Then she rose from her chair and walked to the chalk-line before the fire. The silence was total now.

"To Motherhood," she said distinctly, and deep-sixed the glass. It sounded like a shattering heart.

She turned then and looked at us speculatively, trying to decide whether to cut loose of it.

"I've been here over three months," she said, "and in that time I've had a lot of laughs. But I've seen some real pain, too, and I've seen you boys help the ones that hurt. That man with one leg; the one whose fiancée entered a nunnery, and was too devout to let himself be sad; the ski instructor who'd gone blind; poor Tom Flannery. I've heard much stranger stories, too, and I think if anyone can help me, you can."

I calculate that by now I must have heard at least a hundred people ask for help of one kind or another in Callahan's—it's that kind of a place. I only remember one getting turned down, and he was a special case. We indicated our willingness to help any way we could, and Fast Eddie fetched her a chair and a fresh drink. She had enough composure back to thank him gently; and then she began talking. During her entire narrative, her voice remained flat, impersonal. As though she were giving a history lesson. Her first words explained why.

"It's a long story," she said wearily, "at least it has been for me. An uncommonly long story. It begins on the day of my birth, which is October 25, 1741."

"*Huh?*" said Doc and Long-Drink and I and—loudest of all—Fast Eddie. "You mean 1941," Eddie corrected.

"Who's telling this story? I mean 1741. And if you boys aren't prepared to believe that, maybe I should stop right now."

We thought about it. Compared to some of the things I've heard—and believed—in Callahan's, this was nothing. Come to think, it explained a few things. Those eyes of hers, for instance.

"Sorry, Rachel," Callahan said for all of us. "So you're 232 years old. Go on."

Eddie looked like he'd been hit by a truck. "Sure t'ing," he said bravely. "Sorry I innarupted."

And in the six or seven hours that ensued, Rachel told us the most incredible tale I have ever heard, before or since. I couldn't repeat that tale if I tried; that uncharacteristically impersonal voice seemed to go on forever with its catalog of sorrows, outlining for us the happinesses and heartbreaks of more than two hundred years of active womanhood. You could probably drag it out of me word for word with deep hypnosis, for I never stopped listening, but the sheer length and weight of the narrative seemed to numb my forebrain for indeterminate periods of time; the aggregate memory is largely gone. But different bits and pieces stuck in the minds of each of us, and I compared notes later. Me, for instance, I recall how, when she was describing what it was like to be crammed in a root cellar while a roaring fire overhead ate her first husband—and her first six children—she kept saying over and over again how cramped it was and how frustrating not to be able to straighten up; it struck me that even after all the intervening years her mind continued to dwell on merely physical hurts. Tom Hauptman now, he remembered in detail the business of her second husband, the minister, going mad and killing her next five kids and himself because anyone who refused to age like God intended must be sent by Satan. Tom said what struck him was how little progress churches have made in two hundred years toward convincing people that the unknown is not by definition evil. Long-Drink is a war games nut—he retained the part about the Battle of Lake Champlain in 1814, which claimed her third husband and two more children. Fast Eddie remembers the story of her first days as a whaler's whore in

Nantucket because she stopped in the middle and asked him solicitously if she was shocking him. ("Not *me*," he said defiantly, "I'll bet you wuz a *terrific* whore!" and she smiled and thanked him and continued, clinically, dispassionately.) Spud Montgomery recalls the three children that resulted from Rachel's whoring years, because Spud's from Alabama and never stopped fighting the Civil War and that's what they died in. Tommy Janssen remembers her last child, the imbecile, who never did learn to feed himself and took thirty-five long years to die, because Tommy grew up with a retarded sister. Doc Webster's strongest memory is of the final birthing, her first in a hospital, the still-born—after which the OB performed the hysterectomy. Doc identified strongly with the astonishment of a doctor faced with a patient in her late twenties whose uterus had delivered eighteen kids. Callahan characteristically recalls the man she was married to at the time, the first man since her psychotic minister to whom she felt she could tell the truth, with whom she did not have to cosmetically "age" herself, with whom she could share her lonely, terrible secret; the gentle and strangely understanding man who cured her of her self-loathing and self-fear and accepted her for what she inexplicably was; the good and loving man who had been killed, mugged for the dollar and a half in his pocket, a month or two before Rachel found Callahan's Place.

But not one of us retains anything like the complete text of Rachel's story. We wouldn't want to if we could, for condensing it into a comprehensibility would turn it into a soap opera. And, probably, we couldn't if we tried. If somebody gave me a guaranteed-accurate rundown of my own *future* in that kind of depth, I don't think I'd remember much more. It was one king hell mountain of a tale, and it displaced its own weight in alcohol as the hours of its telling dragged by.

Me, I'm thirty-five years old, and I have been there and

back again, and when Rachel finished her virtually unin-
terrupted narration I felt like a five-year-old whose great-
grandmother has just recited the Story of Her Life in
horrific detail.

In the dead silence that grew from Rachel's last words
there just didn't seem to be anything to say to her, no
words in all my experience that wouldn't sound banal
—like telling a leper that it's always darkest before the
dawn. Not that there had been agony in her voice at any
time during her recital, nor any on her face when she
finished. That was the most ghastly thing about her tale; it
was delivered with the impersonal detachment of an his-
torian, recited like the biography of one long dead. You
Are There At The Battle of Lake Champlain.

Oh, there was pain aplenty in her story, sure—but so
buried, under two centuries of scars, that it could only be
inferred. And yet the pain *had* been there earlier, had
broken through to the surface for a moment at least, when
Rachel had cried. How? Why?

I became peripherally aware of the men of Callahan's
Place, arrayed around me with their mouths open. Even
Callahan looked pole-axed—and that almost scared me. I
glanced around, looking for even one face that held some
kind of answer, some kind of consolation, some word for
Rachel.

And found one. Fast Eddie's mouth was trembling, but
there were words in it struggling to get out. He couldn't
seem to bring himself to speak, but he looked like he sure
and hell wanted to.

Callahan saw it too. "You look like you got something
to say, Eddie," he said gently.

Eddie seemed to reach a decision all at once. Whirling
to face Callahan, he jammed his hands in his hip pockets
and snarled—snarled!—"Who ast you? I got *nuttin'* to
say."

Callahan started, and if I'd had any capacity for shock left I'd have been shocked. *Eddie* barking at Callahan? It was like watching Lassie sink her fangs into Tommy's leg.

"Eddie," Doc Webster began reasonably, "if you have any words that might help Rachel here I think you ought to . . ."

"SHADDAP!" Eddie blared. "I tell ya I got nuttin' ta say, see?"

The silence returned, and stayed a while. We could only surmise that Rachel's tale of sorrow had unhinged the banty little piano player. Creeping Jesus, it had near unhinged me—and I wasn't in love with her. The central issue, then, was still Rachel. Well . . . if Eddie had nothing to say, who did?

Who else?

"So all you have left is immortality, eh Rachel?" Callahan rumbled. "Tough break."

That did seem to put a little perspective on it. Surely Rachel's run of bad luck was due to change soon. It was only logical. "Sure, Rachel," I said, beginning to cheer up. "You're bound to start getting the breaks anytime now."

But it was no good. There was a smile on her face, but not a happy one.

"It figures," Long-Drink said hurriedly. "You can have a run of bad cards that seems to last forever, but sooner or later you pick up your hand and find four aces. It's just the Law of Averages, Rachel. Things always even out in the end."

"Sorry boys," Rachel said, still smiling sadly. "Nice try. I understand what you're saying—but there are a couple of holes in the logic. Two incorrect assumptions, one of them your mistake and one of them mine."

"What mistakes?" Callahan asked, his rugged face wrinkled in thought.

"Your mistake first, Mike. It's a natural one, I suppose, but it's a mistake just the same. What makes you think I'm immortal?"

"Eh?"

"I'm older than any four of you put together, yes. But longevity is not immortality. Mike, *nothing* is immortal: ask Dorian Gray. My clock runs as slow as his did—but it runs."

"But you . . ."

". . . look a lot younger than 232 years old," she finished. "Right. I look like I'm maybe crowding thirty. But Mike: *what's my natural lifespan?*"

He started to answer, than shut up, looking thoughtful. Who the hell knew?

"Someday I will die," Rachel went on, "just like you, like Tom Flannery. Like all humans; like all living things. I *know* that, I feel it in my bones. And there isn't a geriatrics expert in the world who can say when. There are no data to work with; as far as I know I am unique."

"I reckon you're right," Callahan conceded, "but so what? Anyone in this room could die tomorrow—we're all under sentence of death, like you said. But to stay sane a body just has to live as though they'll go on forever, assume there's a lot of years left. Hellfire, Tom Flannery lived that way, and he *knew* better. Maybe there ain't no way to figure the odds for you—but if I was an insurance salesman, I'd love to have your business. Jake and Long-Drink are right: there's good times around the corner, always, and I bet you live to see 'em.

"I may not be as old as you, Rachel, but there's one thing I've learned in the time I have been around: joy always equals pain in the long run."

She shook her head impatiently and sighed. "The second mistake, Mike. The one that's my fault, in a way. You see, the most spectacular points of the story I've told you all tonight are the bad times, and so it must seem like I've just always been a hard-luck kid. But that's not so at all. I've known happiness too, in full measure, with Jacob and Isaiah and even with Benjamin, and most of all with my second and most beloved Jacob. There were good times in Nantucket if it comes to that, and throughout the whoring years; the profession is vastly underrated. And my joys have been greater, I think, than any of you could know —because you are correct, Mike: joy is the product of the pain that has gone before it, and vice versa. I know I could never have appreciated Jacob's quiet acceptance as much if I hadn't been looking for it for two centuries.

"Oh, the seesaw never stops, I learned that when Jacob was killed—but then again I was gladder to find this bar than any customer you've ever had."

"Then what . . . I mean, why uh . . .?"

"Why am I hurting? Hear me, Mike: there is nothing like extended life to make you aware that you're going to die someday. I am more aware of my own mortality than any of you could possibly be. Damn it, I've been dying for two hundred years!

"And how do you, how do normal people come to terms with that awareness of mortality? How do *you* beat death?"

"Oh lord," the Doc gasped. "I remember now. That toast . . ."

"Yes." Rachel nodded. "The one that gave me the weeps, for the first time in twenty years. 'To Motherhood.' I don't want to see or hear or say anything about motherhood ever again! A man or woman who's afraid of dying will either decide to believe in an afterlife . . . or have children, so that something of himself or herself will live on. I haven't believed in God since my years with Benjamin—and all my babies died childless and I can't have any more! I had nineteen chances at real immortality, and they all came up craps. I'm the last of my line.

"So what will I leave behind me? I haven't the gift to

leave great books or paintings or music; I can't build anything; I have no eternal thoughts to leave the world. I've been alive longer than anyone on Earth—and when I'm gone I'll leave *nothing;* nothing more durable than your memories of me.''

Her voice had begun to rise shrilly; her hands danced in her lap. ''For awhile I had hope, for those of my children who shared my birthmark—an hourglass on its side, high on the left shoulderblade—seemed to have a genetic share in my longevity. But that damned birthmark is a curse, an unbeatable hex. Not one of the marked children had any interest at all in siring or bearing children of their own, and accident or illness cut them down, every one. If even one of them had left a child, I could die happy. But the curse is unbroken,'' she slammed her fist down on the bar. ''When I go I'll be *gone*, solid gone without a trace. Centuries of living, and no heritage more durable than a footprint in the snow!''

She was crying again, her voice strident and anguished, contorted with pain. I could see Eddie, his own face twisting with strong emotion, trying to break in; but now that he wanted to talk she wouldn't let him.

''So what have you got to offer me, boys? What's your solution? Have you got anything more useful than four fingers of bourbon?'' She got up and flung her empty glass at the fireplace, began grabbing glasses off the bar and throwing them too, grunting with effort, still speaking: ''*What* kind of . . . *an*-swers have you . . . *got* for an . . . *old* old lady who's . . . *trapped* in a moving . . . *box* sliding . . . *downhill* to . . .'' She had run out of glasses, and with the last words she gripped the long-legged armchair she'd been sitting on and heaved it high over her head to throw it too into the fire, and as she stood there with the heavy chair held high her face changed, a look of enormous puzzlement smoothing over the hysterical rage.

". . . death?" she finished softly, and crumpled like a rag doll, the chair bouncing and clattering into a corner.

The Doc was fast, and ten feet closer, but Fast Eddie beat him easily. He slid the last yard on his knees, lifted Rachel's head with great tenderness onto his lap, and hollered, "Rachel, *lissen* ta me!" The Doc tried to take her away from him, and Eddie backhanded him off his feet without looking up. "Lissen ta me Rachel, LISSEN goddamn it!" he thundered.

Her eyes fluttered open. "Yes, Eddie."

"Ya can't die, Rachel, not yet. You go and die on me an' I'll break both your arms, I swear to God. Lissen here, *if you want a daughter I can fix it.*"

She smiled, a faint and bitter smile. "Thanks, Eddie, but adoption just isn't the same."

"I ain't talkin' about adoption," he barked. "But I tell ya I can fix it. Ida spoke up sooner, but you said you didn't ever want to think about kids again. Now will ya lissen, or are you too busy dyin'?"

She was teetering on the edge, but I guess curiosity must be a powerful stimulant. "What . . . what do you mean?"

"I'm sterile too, damn it. My wife divorced me for it." Our eyes widened a little more at this revelation, and I was suddenly ashamednof how little I knew about Eddie. "But I kept my ears open an' I found out how to beat it, how ta leave somethin' behind, see? Did you ever hear of cloning?"

She looked startled. "You can't clone people, Eddie."

"Not today, you can't. Maybe you an' I won't live to see it happen, either. But I can take ya inta Manhattan to a place where they'll freeze a slice o' yer skin, a lousy coupla million cells, an' keep 'em on ice 'til they *can* clone people. Tom Flannery's there now, frozen like a popsicle, waitin' for 'em to invent a cure for leukemia; he tol' me about it.''

I gasped in astonishment; saw Callahan beginning a broad grin.

''So how 'bout it, Rachel?'' Eddie snapped. ''You want cryonics? Or d'ya just wanna cry?''

She stared at Eddie for a long moment, focusing about five feet past him, and nobody dared exhale. And then two centuries of fighting spirit came through, and she smiled, a genuine smile of acceptance and peace.

''Thank you, Eddie,'' she breathed. Her eyes became for one timeless instant the eyes of a young girl, the eyes that belonged on that youthful face; and then they closed, and she began to snore softly. Rachel, who mourned for her lost children, and was comforted.

Doc Webster got up off the floor, checked her pulse, and slapped Eddie on the back. ''Always a pleasure, *herr doktor*, to assist you in the technique which bears your name,'' he said jovially, spitting out a tooth. ''Your medicine is stronger than mine.''

Eddie met his gaze a little awkwardly, started to pick up Rachel's sleeping form, and then paused. ''Gimme a hand, will ya, Doc?''

''Sure thing, buddy. We'll take her over to Smithtown General for observation, but I think she'll be OK.'' Together they lifted her gently and headed for the door.

But Eddie stopped when they reached it and turned toward Callahan, staring at the floor. ''Mike,'' he began. ''I . . . Uh . . . what I mean . . .'' The apology just wouldn't come.

Callahan laughed aloud for the sheer joy of it and pegged the stump of his cigar into the fireplace. ''You guys,'' he said, shaking his head. ''Always cloning around.''

8

Unnatural Causes

There's been a lot of noise in the papers lately about the series of seismic shocks that have been recorded over the last few weeks in the unlikeliest places. Quake-predicting is a young art, from what I hear, and an occasional freak disturbance now and again should be no real cause for alarm—but an unpredicted miniquake every day for two or three weeks, spotted all around the globe, culminating in a blockbuster where a quake had no right to be, is bound to cause talk.

The seismologists confess themselves baffled. Some note that none of the quakes took place in a densely populated area, and are somewhat reassured. Some note the uniquely powerful though strictly local intensity of the blasts, and are perturbed. Some note the utter inability of their science to explain the quakes even after the fact, and fear that the end of the world is at hand.

But me—well, from here at the site of the first quake in the series, Suffolk County, Long Island, New York, U.S.A., I've got me a different idea.

If you've been paying attention so far, you probably know what a circus Callahan's Place can be on an ordinary night. Well I'm here to tell you that on holidays like Christmas and New Year's Eve, it becomes something to stagger the imagination. All the stops are pulled out, insanity reigns supreme, and the joint generally resembles a cross between a Shriner's Convention and an asylum run by the Marx Brothers.

So perhaps it wasn't surprising that the first quake in the series struck damn near Callahan's Place on Halloween Eve. It certainly couldn't have happened the way it did on any other night.

The place was more packed than even I had ever seen it before, and I've been hanging out at Callahan's for quite a few years now. Added to the usual list of regulars and semi-regulars were a host of old-timers and ex-regulars, some of whom I knew only by reputation and some not at all. As I think I already told you, a lot of Callahan's customers stop needing to drink after they've been around long enough, and not many people in this crazy age enjoy judicious doses of ethanol for its own sake. So they stop showing up, or become more involved with their families, or simply move elsewhere—but holidays somehow draw them all back like chickens to the roost come sundown.

So by nine o'clock Callahan had already had to sweep the shattered glasses out of the fireplace to make way for incoming shipments, leaving Tom Hauptman to cover the bar, and more people were coming in all the time.

Nearly everyone had come in costume, lending a surreal air to a bar that's never been what you'd call mundane. There were four guys in gorilla suts playing poker in the corner, five or six sheeted ghosts doing a shuffle-off-to-Buffalo through the press of the crowd, and seventeen assorted bug-eyed monsters and little green men scattered here and there. I was profoundly glad to see that Eddie had finished his mourning and put away his grief; he had showed up in black-face and the most disheveled suit I'd ever seen, announcing, "I'm Scott Joplin—lookit my rags." Doc Webster had dressed up as Hippocrates and was instantly dubbed "Hippo-Crates" (having been forced to use a tarpaulin for a toga); Long-Drink McGonnigle appeared in an ancient frock-coat with a quill pen in the breast pocket, introducing himself as "Balzac—Balz to you;" Noah Gonzalez and Tommy Janssen had teamed up as a horse with a head at both ends because neither of them wanted to be the . . . aw, you get the idea. Callahan himself was dressed up as a grizzly bear, which suited his huge Irish bulk well, but he kept wincing when jostled, explaining to anyone foolish enough to listen that he was "a b'ar tender." Me, I was dressed as a pirate with a black eye-patch and the name of a certain oil company painted across my chest.

I was watching the tumult and enjoying myself hugely, trying to guess the identity of friends through their masks, when I spotted one very familiar face unmasked.

It was Mickey Finn.

I hadn't seen Finn for quite a spell, since he moved up to the Gaspé Peninsula in Canada to do some farming, and I was delighted to see that he'd made the reunion.

"Finn!" I hollered over the merry roar. "This way."

Another human might not have heard me, but Finn looked up right away, smiled across the room at me, and started working his way toward the bar.

There's some machine in Finn, the way he tells it, but I think there's a lot of human in him too. He could easily have put a hand through the wall, but he was extremely careful not to discommode anyone on his way to the bar. I looked him over as he approached, noted his work shirt, sturdy coveralls and worn boots, and decided he was making a fair adjustment to his life of exile as a Terran. Wrinkles on either side of his smile said that it was no longer such an alien expression to him as it had once been.

He reached me at last, shook my hand gravely and accepted a glass of rye from Tom Hauptman. He offered Tom the traditional one-dollar bill.

"No thanks, Mr. Finn," Tom told him. "Mike says your money's no good here."

Finn smiled some more, kept the bill extended. "Thank you, sir," he said in that funny accent of his, "but I truly prefer to pay my own way."

I shook my head. "If you're gonna be human, Finn, you're gonna have to learn to accept gifts," I told him.

He sobered up and put away his money, nodding to himself as much as to me. "Yes. This is a hard learning, my friend. I must not refuse a gift from Mr. Callahan, who gave me the greatest gift—my free will."

"Hey, Finn, don't take it so hard," I said quickly. "Accepting a gift graciously is something a lot of humans never learn. Why should you be more human than Spiro Agnew?" I leaned back against the bar and took a sip of Bushmill's. "Come on, loosen up. You're among friends."

Finn looked around, his shoulders relaxing. "Some of these are unfamiliar to me," he said, gesturing toward the crowd.

"Lot's of 'em are strangers to me too," I said. "Let's amble around and get to know some of 'em. But first, tell me what you've been doing with yourself. How's life in Canada?"

"I am doing well," Finn said, "and I am also doing good, I think."

"How do you mean?"

"Jake my friend," Finn said earnestly, "the Gaspé is one of the biggest paradoxes on this continent: some of the richest farmland, and some of the poorest farmers. In addition to making my own living, I have been trying to help them."

"How do you do that?" I asked, interested.

"In small ways," Finn replied. "I see further into the infrared than their eyes can see; I can evaluate soil at a glance and compute yield, evaluate their growing crops much better than they, suggest what to plan for. That taught them to listen to my opinions, and of late I have been speaking of the necessity for alternate means of distributing their goods. It goes slowly—but one day those frozen acres will feed many hungry people, I hope.''

"Why, that's just fine, Finn," I said, slapping him on the back. "I knew there was work for a man like you. Come on, let's meet some of the old-timers." Finn, being as tight with his words as some gents are with their money, nodded briefly and we plunged into the thick of the crowd.

I spotted four tables pushed together near the fireplace, at which were seated the Doc, Sam Thayer, and a whole bunch of apparent strangers in assorted odd costumes. Best of all, Callahan was standing nearby—it seemed like a great place to start. I steered Finn in that direction, collecting a couple of chairs on the way and signalling Callahan to join us. When he saw Finn his face lit with pleasure, and he nodded.

As we sat down, one of the unfamiliar gents, dressed as a shepherd, was just finishing a plaintive rendition of "I Know I'll Never Find Another Ewe," and was applauded by a chorus of groans and cat-calls.

"Better take it on the lamb, Tony," Doc Webster suggested.

"Where there's a wool, Thayer's away," agreed Sam, rising as if to leave. One of the boys removed his chair with a thoughtful expression, and he sat back down rather farther than he had intended. Callahan lumbered up and appropriated the chair, the head of his bear-costume under his arm, and Sam promptly sat on Bill Gerrity's lap. This is funnier than it sounds, because Bill is a transvestite and was done up as Marilyn Monroe that particular night (while Callahan's is certainly not the only bar where Bill can indulge his peculiarity, it's the only one where he doesn't have to put up with the annoyance of being propositioned regularly—and Bill is *not* gay). As Sam was dressed as Mortimer Snerd, the effect was spectacular, and those around the room not otherwise occupied cheered and whistled. One of the gorillas in the corner looked up from his cards and scowled.

I glanced around the table, taking inventory: a fireman, a five-foot-seven duck, two bug-eyed monsters (one purple and tentacled, one green and furry) and one Conan the Barbarian. "Hey Mike," I called to Callahan, "introduce me and Finn around and we'll swap stories." Callahan nodded and opened his mouth, but the Doc put a beer in front of it. "I bear beer, bear," he announced, and another groan arose.

"Okay," I said. "I'll start the ball rollin' myself. Howdy folks, I'm Jake. This here's Mickey Finn." Various hellos came from the group, and a pretzel landed in my drink.

"I've heard of you, Mr. Finn," said the shepherd, grinning. "They say you're hell to drink with."

Obviously the shepherd hadn't heard about *this* Mickey Finn, and I glanced at Finn to see how he'd take it. I needn't have worried—apparently he had been hanging around Callahan's Place long enough.

"You'll make me feel sheepish, sir," he said with a straight face, "if you take my name too litter-ally. Very baa-adly indeed, for I would feign have fun with a fine Finn fan."

Callahan and I guffawed, and Doc Webster's jaw dropped. "Lord God," the Doc expostulated, "I'm going to hang up my puns, I swear."

"A hypocritic oath," said the duck, and the Doc heaved a bag of beer nuts at him. "Duck, duck, the Doc," Callahan and I crowed together, and the table broke up.

"Look Jake," said the shepherd when the commotion had died down, "what you said about swapping stories sounds good to me. As we introduce ourselves, let's explain what brought us here to Callahan's. I know some of you boys must have stories I'd like to hear—nobody seems to come here without a reason. What do you say?"

We all looked around. "Suits." "Okay by me." "Why not?" There was no apparent reluctance—Callahan's is the place you went to first because you needed to talk about your troubles—and the first time is always the hardest. "Fine," said the shepherd. "I guess I ought to start." He took a glass, filled it up and wetted his whistle. He was about my age, with odd streaks of white hair on either temple that combined with his classical shepherd's garb made him look like a young Homer. His features were handsome and his build excellent, but I noted with surprise that his left earlobe was missing. There was a scar on his right shoulder, nearly hidden by a deep tan, that looked like it had been put there with a crosscut saw.

"My name is Tony Telasco," he said when he had swallowed. "I give lectures and slide shows and make speeches, and sometimes I go to jail, but I used to do a lot of things before I came to Callahan's. I was a transcendental meditator for awhile, staring at my navel. Before that I was a junkie, and before that I was a drunk and before that I was a killer. That was right after I was a kid.

"See, the thing I *really* am is a Viet Nam veteran."

There were low whistles and exclamations all around.

I was in my first year of college (Tony went on) when I got that magic piece of paper from my draft board. Business Ad majors just weren't getting deferments, and so I had the classic three choices: go to jail, Canada, or Viet Nam.

Which wasn't a lot of choice. Make no mistake, I was scared spitless of Viet Nam—I watched television. But I was scared and ashamed to go to jail, and scared and incompetent to emigrate. To be brought into a strange country to fight would be tough, but to move into one myself and make a living with no skills and no degree looked impossible to me.

So Nam seemed to be the lesser of three evils. I never

made a moral decision about the war, never questioned whether going there was the right thing to do. *It was the easiest*. Oh, I knew a few guys who went to Canada, but I never really understood them—I liked America. And I knew one fellow in my English class who went to jail for refusing to step forward—but his third day there they found him on the end of his bedsheet, a few inches off the floor, his cellmate apparently asleep.

And so I found myself in the Army. Basic was tough, but tolerable; I'd always liked physical exercise, and I was in pretty good shape to start with. It was a lot rougher on my mind.

The best friend I made in Basic was a guy named Steve McConnell, from California. Steve was a good joe, the kind of guy really good to have with you in a rugged situation like Basic. He had a knack for pointing out the idiocies of military life, and a huge capacity for enjoying them. Kind of a dry sense of humor—he didn't laugh out loud, in fact he hardly ever laughed *aloud*, but he was perpetually amused by things that drove me crazy. Like me, he'd sort of drifted into the Army, but the more he thought about the idea, the less he liked it. Neither did I, but I didn't see anything I could do about it. We spent hours peeling potatoes together, discussing war and women and the Army and women and the Communist Menace in Southeast Asia and women and our D.I. Steve was an independent thinker—he didn't hang out with the other blacks in our outfit, who had cliqued up in self-protection. That can be tough for a black man in the U.S. Army, but Steve cut his own path, and chose his brothers by other criteria than the shade they were painted. I don't know why he and I were so tight—I don't know what his criteria were—but somehow we were so close I got the idea I really knew him, understood where he was at.

I was as surprised as anyone when he finally made his stand.

There comes a day, see, when they line you up on a godawful cold February morning and truck up a couple of coffin-sized cartons. The D.I.'s are clearly more pretentious than usual, projecting the air that something sacred is about to happen. By Army standards they're right.

What happens is, you get to the head of the line and throw out your hands and one huge mother of a sergeant flings a rifle at you as hard as he can—you've been Issued Your Rifle, and mister, God have mercy on you if you drop it, or fumble your catch and let part of it touch the ground. Worse than calling it a "gun." A few guys do catch copper-plated hell for having fingers too frozen to clutch, and you spend your time on line furiously flexing your fingers and praying to God you won't blow it.

Steve was right in front of me in line, and curiously withdrawn; I couldn't get a rise out of him with even the sourest joke. I chalked it up to the cold and the solemnity of the occasion, and I guess I was part right.

All at once it was his turn and the big sergeant selected a rifle and pressed it to his chest and straightarmed it with a bit extra oomph because he was from Alabama and I prayed Steve would field it okay and he just simply sidestepped.

It was just like that: one rushing second and then time stopped. Steve pulled to his left and the rifle cartwheeled past him and struck earth barrel-first, *sank* a motherloving three inches into the mud, the stock brushing my knee. All around the parade ground people stopped cursing and joking and stared, stared at that damned M-1 quivering in the mud like a branch planted by an idiot, stared and waited for the sky to fall.

The big sergeant got redder than February wind could

account for and swelled up like a toad, groping for an obscenity that could contain his fury. As he found it, Steve spoke up in the mildest voice I ever heard.

"I'm sorry, sergeant," he said, "but I can't take that rifle."

The sergeant glared at him a long moment, then holstered his .45 and waved over a couple of corporals. "Take this goddamn nigger to the guardhouse," he snarled, and bent over the carton again. Before I had time to think he heaved a rifle at me, and I made a perfect catch. "Next!" he bellowed, and the line moved forward. I found myself in barracks, looking at my new rifle and wondering why Steve had done such a crazy thing. Steve's navel. "This thing kills too, *private*. Pick up that rifle."

I looked at Steve, paralyzed by his crazy stunt. He was plainly scared to death, and I was as sure as he that he was about to die. *Pick it up, Steve*, I prayed. *You don't have to use it now, just pick the goddamned thing up.*

"Sergeant," he said finally, "you can make me pick it up, but you can't *ever* make me use it. Not even with that automatic. So what's the point?"

The sergeant glared at him a long moment, then holstered his .45 and waved over a couple of corporals. "Take this goddamn nigger to the guardhouse," he snarled, and bent over the carton again. Before I had time to think he heaved a rifle at me, and I made a perfect catch. "Next!" he bellowed, and the line moved foreard. I found myself in barracks, looking at my new rifle and wondering why Steve had done such a crazy thing.

I went off to Nam soon after that—tried to get word to Steve in the stockade, but it couldn't be done. He got left behind with the rest of America, and I found myself in a jungle full of unfriendly strangers. It was bad—real bad—and I began to think a lot about Steve and the choice he had made. I couldn't tell the people I was fighting from the people I was fighting for, and the official policy of "kill what moves" didn't satisfy me.

At first. Then one day a twelve-year-old boy as cute as Dondi took off my left earlobe with a machete while I got some K-rations out of my pack for him. The kid would have taken off my head instead of my ear, but a pretty tight buddy of mine, Sean Reilly, shot him in the belly while he was winding up.

"Christ, Tony," Sean said when he'd made sure the kid was dead, "you know the word: never turn your back on a Gook."

I was too busy with my bleeding ear to reply, but I was coming to agree with him. Just as Nam had been easier than jail, catching the rifle easier than refusing to, killing Gooks was easier than discussing political philosophy with them.

A week later it got to be more than easy.

Sean's squad had been sent upriver to reconnoiter, while the rest of us got our breath back for the big push. I was on sentry duty with a fellow whose name I misremember—not a bad guy, but he smoked marijuana, and I'd been raised to think that stuff was evil. Anyway this particular day he smoked a couple of joints while we sat there listening to jungle sounds and waiting for relief so we could eat. It made him thirsty, so I offered to spell him while he went to the river for a drink. He slipped into the jungle, walking a little unsteadily.

A minute later I heard him scream.

It was only fifty yards or so to the river, but I came circumspectly, expecting to find him dead and the enemy in strength. But when I poked my rifle through the foliage, there was nobody in sight but him. He was on his knees with his face buried in his hands. *Oh Jesus*, I thought, *what a time to freak out*. I started to swear at him, and then I saw what he had seen.

It was Sean, floating lazily against the bank with his

fingers and toes dangling from a sort of necklace around his throat and his genitals sewed into his mouth.

A friend, a man who had saved my life, a guy who wanted to be an artist when he got home, carved up like a Christmas turkey by a bunch of slant-eye monkeys—it became much more than easy to kill Gooks.

It became fun.

The rest of my tour passed in a red haze. I remember raping women, I remember clubbing a baby's skull with a rifle-butt to encourage a V.C.-sympathizer to talk, I remember torturing captured prisoners and enjoying it. I remember a dozen little My Lais, and I remember me in the middle with a smile like a wolf. Fury tasted better than confusion, and this time it was easier to *kill* than to think.

I don't know what would have happened to me if I'd come home kill-crazy like that. God knows what happened to the ones that did. But two weeks before I was due to go home I got a letter from a friend in the States, a supply corporal back at boot camp.

Steve McConnell had died in military prison. He "fell down the stairs" and broke nearly every bone in his body, but it was the ruptured spleen that killed him. There had been no inquiry; the official verdict was "accidental death." As accidental as Sean's—except our side did it.

In the time it took me to read that letter I went from kill-crazy all the way to the other kind, and the next morning I took my squad out and tried to die and loused it up and got my second Purple Heart and Silver Star. I never got another chance in Nam; they sent me home from the hospital with some neat embroidery on this seam on my shoulder and a piece of paper that said I was a normal human being again.

Killing myself just didn't seem as reasonable in the States as it had in Nam somehow, so I tried forgetting instead. For a while booze did the trick, but I couldn't keep it up; my stomach wouldn't tolerate the dosage required. Then for a while pot was a real help, but some ways made it worse: visions of spurting blood and Sean's fingers and Steve boneless like a jello man. So I tried a hit of coke, and that was just fine, and one day a spade who looked a lot like Steve laid some smack on me. Heroin was just what I'd been looking for, and it wasn't any surprise when I got a Jones, a habit I mean.

But it's funny . . . I guess I really *didn't* want to kill myself at all. I heard about this transcendental meditation stuff and started hanging around Ananada Marga Yoga Society meetings, and boy, I kicked clean. Instead of getting high on smack, I got high on big bites of bliss, which is cheaper, healthier, legal and a much more satisfactory head all the way around.

It was over a year before I noticed I wasn't accomplishing anything.

But about that time I got lucky and took my Doctor Webster's advice and started coming to Callahan's Place. Things started getting clearer in my head, a lot clearer. Next thing I knew, I was on a stage giving a speech to the V.V.A.W., and I learned that there are things worth fighting and fighting for—but fighting clean. I started giving talks and joining demonstrations and appearing on T.V. I've been arrested four times, had my leg broken by a county cop, and they took my name off the Native Sons Honor Roll in my home town. My father won't talk to me—yet—and my phone is tapped.

I feel great.

". . . and it's all thanks to you, Mr. Callahan," Tony finished.

"Shucks, Tony," Callahan rumbled, "we didn't do anything for you that you couldn't have done yourself."

"You accepted me," Telasco said simply. "You made me understand that I was just a normal human being who'd been caught up in a nightmare, a nightmare that made him realize he had the makings of a killer ape in him. One night I told you and your customers this whole story and you didn't stare at me like a mad dog. You told me that I needed a bigger audience.

"You showed me that it wasn't my killer nature that was shameful, but the refusal to think things out that landed me in Nam in the first place. You showed me that just because it took me a while to make the sort of decision Steve made didn't mean that I didn't have Steve's kind of guts in me somewhere. I was sure I didn't have that kind of guts, and so I never looked for them. When I did . . . I found them. Because you had faith in me.

"Jail is no picnic," he told the rest of us, "but I want to do what I can to see that no one else gets caught in the meatgrinder like I did. But I don't do it from guilt. I do it for its own sake." He looked at Callahan. "I already got my absolution here."

Callahan topped off his glass and slapped him on the back. "Well spoke, Tony," he boomed, and we all raised our glasses and toasted him in unison. The fireplace exploded with glass when we were through.

"I knew it," said the Doc, "as soon as I saw him dressed as a shepherd I *knew* he had to be a vet." Groans arose, but the comic relief was timely.

"If you don't pipe down some, Doc, he won't be the only hoarse doctor around here," Callahan attempted.

"Now, now," said the Doc. "I'm a happily married man. I don't fool around with hoarse in either of our professional capacities."

I started to ask if the Doc's capacities were truly professional, but before I could, Mickey Finn grabbed Callahan's shoulder so hard he winced—something nobody else could have managed.

"My friend Mike," Finn said urgently, "That person there, in the green costume—it is not a costume. He is not human."

Callahan blinked, and such jaws as were visible dropped like gallows trapdoors. If anyone but Finn had said that—anywhere but Callahan's Place—we'd have thought he was crazy or drunk.

"I see further into the infrared range than you humans," Finn went on hurriedly. "I was watching the currents of heat from the fireplace make patterns in the air while I listened to your words, enjoying their lazy beauty . . . but I just caught the green one watching them too. Close examination shows me that his fur and features are genuine. Friends, this is an alien."

We all stared at the green fellow, waiting for him to take off his mask and say something. He *looked* human enough—the usual number of arms and legs I mean. His mouth was a trifle too wide, now that I noticed, and the fur sure looked awful real. If those pointed, oversized ears were glued on, I couldn't see where.

He looked back at us, put down his glass and shrugged knobby, tufted shoulders. "There is no point in denying it, gentlemen. I am not human. In fact, I came here tonight specifically to tell you how unhuman I am. The words I have heard encouraged me to confess, but still I . . . hesitated. However, now that I have been identified by another non-human, I suppose I must speak. Will you listen?"

Callahan spoke for all of us. "Mister, if you've got troubles, you're in the right place. Go ahead."

The green alien nodded. His eyes were deeply troubled.

"My name, gentlemen," he said in a pleasing tenor, "is Broodseven-Sub-Two Raksha, as well as it can be translated into your tongue. I am . . . well, the profession does not really exist as such here, but my function combines elements of sociologist, psychologist, soldier and farmer. My people are the Krundai, and Krundar my home is located so far from here that your instruments have not yet detected its sun. There are several dozen Krundai on your planet, a team which has been here for over two thousand years . . . a team of which I am the least member." He paused, looked embarrassed.

"What are you fellers doin' here?" Callahan asked.

"That," said the alien hesitantly, "is what I have come here to tell you. It is . . . it is not an easy thing to tell. I have spent almost thirty of your years formulating my opinions in words and seeking someone to whom to speak them. Fifteen of those years sufficed to eliminate as confidantes all of my fellow Krundai; for another ten I debated whether I could conceivably unburden myself to a human. Unable to resolve the question, I spent the last five years picking those humans in whom I *might* confide. I found on your planet a total of only two or three thousand humans who I felt might be able to understand and help, and thirty-five of those are now present in this room.

"All of you at this table are such."

We looked around at each other, wondering whether we were all special or just crazy in the same way. I sure didn't feel special.

"Even now," Raksha went on, "I have not entirely resolved my debate. My decision is much like that of Mr. Telasco, but it is further complicated in that it could involve betraying my entire race. The presence of Mr. Finn, whom I find to be, as he says, as non-human as myself, complicates things considerably—although I suspect his origins may better enable him to empathize with me."

He faced Finn. "Space holds many viewpoints, Finn. You seem to be a traveler, of broader experience than these ephemerals. Will you try to understand me?"

Finn looked him square in the eye. "I will listen."

Raksha didn't seem to care much for that answer, but he nodded. He turned to us. "Will you . . . all of you . . . swear that no word of what I tell you will reach my fellow Krundai? I must warn you that confiding in other humans would accomplish this thing."

This time there was no more need for us to look around than there was for all of us to speak. "Every man at this table can keep his lip buttoned," Callahan said simply. "Speak your piece."

The green furry alien looked us all over one last time, one after the other, beginning and ending with Callahan. As his eyes met mine, I noticed for the first time that the surfaces of them rippled with faintly glistening semicircular lines, just like the one you look for when you're pouring coffee into a dark cup. They shifted position in a different way than the specks on a human eyeball do, independent of the motion of the eyes themselves. They scared the hell out of me somehow, more than the fur and the ears did.

He reached his decision.

"Yes, gentlemen, you are right. Come what may, I must speak. If I can be helped by any one, of any race, it is you. Brood help me if you cannot."

I grabbed a pitcher and got half of it down before Bill and Sam snatched it away.

"I must begin," the alien went on, "by explaining to you some central facts about my people.

"First, we live much, much longer than humans. An average Krundai sees his three-thousandth birthday before returning to the Great Pouch, and some have lived as much as five or six centuries longer. I myself am well over eight hundred years old, and I am the youngest Krundai on your world, having been born here."

"That explains how you know our language and idiom so well," I interrupted.

"My four immediate ancestors had a hand in its creation," Raksha said drily.

I shut up.

"Second, as you may well imagine, we are a very patient people, by your standards. Even allowing for the difference in our respective life-spans, we move in much less haste than you, and plan projects in terms of how many of our generations they will require to complete. Our concern is for the continuing life of the race, rather than our individual lives, as the Broodmaster has decreed.

"Third, we have an ingrained loathing for killing or violence."

That cheered me quite a bit, although I don't think I was really scared with Finn around. That guy could maybe use this Earth to light a cigar with if he had a mind to. Besides, if the Krundai had intended us harm, it seemed to me they'd have done so centuries ago.

"We realize," Raksha went on, "that such things must be: the prime datum of the Universe is that life survives by eating life, and no other way. The expense of eating is, in great part, the resistance the second life offers to being eaten. For instance, the roast-beef sandwiches you have provided for your friends, Mr. Callahan (and by the way they are easily the thickest I have ever seen in a tavern) are currently quite expensive, because of the size and unwieldiness of the system required to supply them to us.

"Suppose you could induce the cow to come here and drop obligingly dead next to your chopping block?

"Still, there are always some who prefer not to do their own butchering. No Krundai will do so voluntarily if it can be avoided. A surprising percentage of your own society, with all your heritage of murder, would like to believe that Life survives by going to the supermarket. So the ideal would be to train cattle to make butcher knives and take turns cutting each other up at a convenient location."

I didn't like the turn this story was taking.

"Which brings me to the fourth significant fact about my people. We have made an exact science of sociopsychology, both Krundai and animal, and refined it beyond your imagining. The closest things you have to it, I suppose, are what you call mob psychology and the actuarial tables your insurance companies use, and you do not even know why they work. The principles behind them, however, are universal, and part of a grand picture which your race will probably never perceive. One of your great writers invented something akin to it called 'psychohistory,' but even that unfulfilled daydream pales beside our knowledge—for psychohistory worked only for humans, and could not predict the appearance of genius or mutation. We can manipulate any sentient race that lives, produce geniuses to order by manipulating society's laboratory conditions; and the nature and causation of mutation are fundamentals of Krundai psychology.

"Of course, like psychohistory, our science works best in the mass, imperfectly with regard to individuals. You humans are at least aware of that supreme paradox—that free will exists to an extent for the individual, but disappears in the group—although you can't work with it. Brood!—you haven't even learned how to measure emotion yet. But we can predict the effects of even one man's *actions* on the society as a whole . . . and we know how to bring about the effects we desire, large scale or small, long run or short.

"Which leaves only one more basic attribute of my people: we are very, very hungry."

I had a ghastly feeling I knew what was coming next, and I didn't like it. The horrible suspicion that Raksha's words were building in my brain answered far too many questions I'd never been satisfactorily able to explain to myself before.

"So that's how that guy got elected," Callahan breathed, and I winced.

"Precisely," Raksha agreed. "You begin to understand why I am here."

"Lay it out, brother," Tony said grimly. "I think I get it, but I hope I'm wrong."

Raksha spread his hands. ''Very simply, gentlemen, for nearly two thousand years your planet has been a Krundai game preserve.''

''God bless my soul,'' said Doc Webster. I looked at Callahan: his face was expressionless, but his eyes were like coals. Tomorrow that table would have inch-deep fingerprints where Finn was holding it.

''For most of that time,'' Raksha continued, ''the Krundai stationed here made no attempt to do more than control your population, inhibit your social evolution and enforce your ignorance. A war here, a philosophical revolution there, discredit a few thinkers and discourage a line of inquiry or two: elementary maintenance. Rome, for instance, got entirely too civilized—even assassinating Caesar didn't help enough. Before long it began to look like they were developing a rudimentary medical science and cutting down the mortality rate.

''So we induced cultural decay, and added some hungry barbarians we found conveniently at hand. An earlier stroke of genius, supplying them with the notion of lead-based waterpipes and wine-vats, paid off handsomely, and the threat was ended.

''We went on in this manner for hundreds of years, allowing just enough growth to preserve vigor and letting you graze freely. We had quite a bit of trouble with plagues—frankly, you're not very clean animals—and finally we decided to let you play with medicine as a simpler solution than running around stamping out an epidemic every few years. There was always war to use as a control and culling device, and anyway, there was plenty of pasture.

''About three hundred years ago, we were notified by Krundar to go into active status and step up production. A food shortage had been predicted, and we were told to expect at any time the order to begin harvesting the herd we had bred and tended so long. We began incubating North America.

"We tripled the usual propaganda to reproduce, filled the continent in an absurdly short time, and encouraged immigration with a massive word-of-mouth advertising campaign about the golden land across the sea, where freedom rang and the streets were paved with gold. It took a bit of finagling to keep Britain from flattening you at the start, but we were in—for us—a hurry. After the requisite wars, we lowered the death-rate considerably to compensate, and began to intensify our efforts.

"A hundred years ago, we received the last command. We have been preparing you to slaughter yourselves ever since."

"Holy Jesus, it figures," Bill Gerrity cried.

"You bet your sweet life it figures," I snarled. "After thousands of years of recorded history, in seventy-five years we go from the Model T Ford to the cobalt bomb and the energy crisis. From corn liquor to Quaaludes. From young giant of a nation to tired old fraud. From . . ."

"Knock it off, Jake," Callahan rapped.

I shut my face. Callahan turned back to Raksha, put his huge meaty hands palm down on the table. "Go on," he said darkly.

The Krundai's fur bristled, and his eyes rolled in his head. Somehow through my rage I understood that this denoted extreme shame in one of his race, and began to cool off, remembering where I was. The air of calm he had worn was shattered now; he was clearly agitated.

"Humans, hear me!" he intoned. "Hear my sins, hear the full catalog of my infamy before you judge. *This is not easy to tell, and I must.*"

"Let him speak," Finn said dispassionately.

"We . . . I and others, I mean . . . instituted an explosive increase of knowledge in the physical sciences, smothered or subverted all the social and spiritual sciences. We cranked your technology to a fever pitch of frenzied production, led you to build yourselves a suicidal ethic and culture, gave you toys like the atom bomb and lysergic acid to play with: we gave a loaded gun to an infant. We manipulated elections and revolutions, staged assassinations, encouraged government to calcify beyond the ability of its people to endure, touched off riots, provided you with news media that would carry the news of growing cancer among you, and did all we could to bring into the minds of men a frustration and a terror that would lead inevitably to chaos. You, the steers, are nearly ready to butcher yourselves for our tables.''

"I don't believe it," the man in the fireman costume burst out. "This is crazy, what you're saying is crazy, just plain nuts. What the hell is this anyway, some kind of a rib?''

"He's serious, Jerry," Callahan said calmly.

"The hell he's serious, Mike, did you hear what he said? You telling me you believe all this stuff?''

"Jerry's right," the duck said. "This guy's nuts.''

"Oh, you fools!" Raksha burst out. "Are you too ignorant to see the pattern? Your whole history makes sense only by positing the four most far-fetched twistings and contradictions to human nature. Use Occam's Razor, by the Brood. Could any race be so suicidal and have lived for this long? Do you really think it accidental that your people went from outhouses to zero-gravity toilets in half a century? From the Merrimac to Skylab in one short century? By our own standards we have turned your planet upside-down in a twinkling—are your lives so short that you have not perceived their acceleration? The pace of progress yanks you ahead faster than you can run. Do you not *notice?*''

Callahan looked across the crowded, oblivious room to Tom Hauptman behind the bar. "Some of us notice," he said softly.

The fireman shook his head. "I don't buy it. That sounds like some crazy sci-fi notion. Conspiracy of aliens my foot, I don't believe in little . . ."

". . . green men?" Raksha finished. "The signs are everywhere around you, Jerry. The squelching of the Air Force's study of unidentified flying objects should have alerted anyone with eyes and ears—save that we had carefully engendered a climate of ridicule and disbelief. We have become more cautious since then. But look beyond the physical evidence: do you believe it blind chance that physics has leaped vast spans while psychology muddled off into blind alleys? Do you really believe man so incurious about himself that it has taken him thousands of years to even begin a science of sociology? Do you think it simply bad luck that the technology of your survival systems, of your food and water and power distribution networks, consistently fail to keep pace with population increase and are already strained to the failing point, even in the face of a technical revolution?

"Does it make sense that after living side by side with natural drugs and hallucinogens of all types for millenia, men have suddenly become dependent on them? Has the worldwide depression, economic and spiritual, escaped you? Does it not surprise you that no language spoken by any people on Earth corresponds with observable reality? Did you think the simultaneous collapse of an ages-old ethical system and a two-century-old value system to be mere unfortunate happenstance? You Broodless fool, *did you really think God died of natural causes?*

"No, my friend. Charles Fort was quite correct: you are property, and on the whole not very bright property. You follow your political and philosophical leaders blindly to the slaughter, grateful to be led, and one in a hundred of you is a Telasco or a McConnell, with the sense to pull out of the mad death-race. You *must* see it, man," he said to Telasco, "you rejected the world we Krundai made for you."

"Jerry," I said, "one of my most precious possessions is a lapel-button, white with black letters. It says 'Go Lemmings Go.' Raksha is telling the truth."

The fireman shook his head like an enraged bull. "This is crazy," he insisted. "How can you be telling us all this? I mean, if you're right, what makes you think we won't tear you to pieces?"

"This is Callahan's Place," the alien said simply. "I am here for absolution."

That brought us all up short, even Jerry. He stiffened; his mouth opened but there were no words in it.

"Why?" cried Doc Webster in agony. "How could a race so old and wise be so savage and murderous?"

"We are *not*," Raksha returned, agony in his own voice. "You kill animals for food—we ourselves have never killed."

"People are not animals," Tony said with quiet force.

"To my people you *are*," insisted the green one. "You lack a . . . an attribute for which there are naturally no words in your tongue. That attribute is central to the Krundai; without it, even if you went to the Great Pouch at the end of your days, you could not suck. To us you are less-than-Krundai. The Sign of the Brood is not upon you: you are food. My people feel no more guilt over engineering your destruction than you would if you could talk a cow into butchering itself."

"Why all this dancing around?" Callahan asked him. "Why not just wipe us out? Sounds to me like you've got the moxie."

"I have told you," Raksha cried. "We abhor violence. The fact that you can be induced to inflict it upon yourselves, is, to us, proof that you are food, less-than-Krundai. If you and other races did not spare us the necessity, we should be forced to kill our own food like beasts. But the Great Brood saw our needs and fashioned the lesser races to breed and feast upon, without the need to nurture violence in our own hearts. First the winged, heat-seeking *fleegh* of Krundar, which fell from the skies into our fires; then the blue-skinned ones of our neighbor planet, who destroyed their atmosphere just before developed interplanetary travel; then the *Krill* from a nearby solar system, who warred to extinction among themselves. It has always been so; it is unforgivably bad form to slay one's own meat oneself. It indicates that one is not in the favor of the Brood.''

"When did your people begin sort of . . . *encouraging* the food into the pot?" Callahan asked.

"So long ago that it would be meaningless to you," Raksha told him. "We learned early that the gifts of the Brood are not free; we must labor for them, to earn a place in the Pouch."

"I still don't see how you could have done it," Jerry said, baffled but obviously believing now, convinced by the pain in the furry alien's voice and the aura of shame around him.

"In the same way that a statesman can be induced to do what he knows is insane," Raksha explained, "by appealing subtly to his own self-interest. We ran a continuous and subtle propaganda campaign, took away any valid reason for living other than personal enrichment and comfort, and then saw to it that the immediate personal interest of millions of people served our ends. One of the simplest methods was to install in an enormous number of people the compulsion to amass more money than they could possibly use: enough were successful to leech national economies into anemia. Another was to whip up an intense interest in sex, far beyond the demands of nature, to keep population-growth beyond your capacity to adapt. Much work was required to squelch interest in space-programs before they could provide an escape valve. You humans are so short-sighted, your lives themselves so short. It is easy to manipulate you.''

"So what changed your mind?" Callahan asked. "You personally, I mean. If we ain't fit for this here Pouch, why are you spilling the beans?"

"I . . . I . . ." he stammered.

"We're nothing but dumb animals, right? Well, Colonel Sanders doesn't apologize to the chickens—*why are you here?*"

The green man groped for words, his pointed ears waving nervously.

"I . . . I don't know," he said at last. "I cannot satisfactorily explain it to myself. There is a climate of belief which runs all through your thought and literature, a conviction that you humans have a higher destiny. This idea has been of use to the Krundai many times, but we did not plan it; it was there when we came. It may be that it is contagious. I do not know; there is something about you humans, a . . . a curious dignity that upsets my heart and troubles my nights."

Finn spoke up, startling me. "I think I know what you mean, friend Raksha," he said in that flat voice of his. "Michael," he went on, turning to Callahan, "do not be so certain that Colonel Sanders does not apologize to his chickens, as you put it. I have myself brought about the extermination of several races, in the days when I served the Masters, and yet last week when I slaughtered my pigs, I grieved for them. They were stupid and dirty and mute—but even a pig may have dignity.

"They did not, could not, comprehend why they died—and yet in an irrational way I wished I could explain it to them." He turned, spoke again to the furry Krundai. "I believe I understand your motivation," he said. "I felt it too, once, and forebore to destroy this world. It seemed a planet of madmen—although much of that appears to be the doing of you and yours. But I knew that not, for you were well-hidden.

"Yet still I stayed the hands of my Masters, betrayed

my purpose, because I learned here in this room that men have love."

"That is the quality I selected for in a human audience," Raksha admitted. "The thing you call love we Krundai had always found to be a symptom of the attribute I spoke of earlier. That humans possess the symptom without the attribute is one of the great anomalies that complicated my thought and delayed my confession until now."

"This propaganda stuff you talked about," Callahan persisted. "I still want to know how you put it across. Whisper in the Wright Brothers' ear? Write newspaper editorials? Spead rumors?"

"Sometimes," Raksha said, and hesitated. His features assumed a deeper green. "And sometimes," he went on with obvious reluctance, "by direct intervention."

"Disguised as humans, you mean? Fifth column and that?" The big Irishman seemed to be prompting, seeking something from Raksha that I couldn't figure out.

"All the Krundai on your world have, at one time or another, impersonated humans for varying reasons. One of us was Saul of Tarsus, another Torquemada, another Thomas Edison. Otto Hahn was yet another."

"And you," Callahan bored on impacably. "Who were *you?*"

I remembered suddenly how long ago Raksha had said he began to regret his job, and my blood went cold as ice.

"I . . ." he said, biting the words off with an effort, "I was known to men as Adolph Hitler."

The silence was a living thing that gnawed at our reason, paralyzed our thought. All around us a Halloween party continued insanely, heedless men laughing and dancing, the four gorillas in the corner playing poker. There was not a damn thing any of us could say, and after a time Raksha went on listlessly, "It was an easy role to play. It took no significant fraction of the training I had received in crowd control. It was so easy that I had time to think, to observe, to learn first-hand what I was doing.

"Perhaps it was because I was born here, and have seen Krundar only once. For whatever reason, I began to doubt; subconscious uncertainty spoiled my work. The major purpose of that campaign was to prolong hostilities long enough to force the development of atomic weapons, and I nearly succeeded in aborting the mission by folding too quickly. But my colleagues were able to redeem my error by drawing out the Pacific conflict just long enough. I told myself my depression was the stigma of personal failure, but I knew in my heart that it was in fact the repair of my mistakes that unsettled me. I have thought on it long and hard since, and now I am here and I have spoken."

Doc Webster produced a hipflask from somewhere on the south slope of his belly, upended it and slapped it down empty. On all sides of us, people drank and chattered and laughed, oblivious to the drama in their midst.

The Doc found his voice someplace; it sounded rusty.

"What do you want from us?" he croaked.

"Absolution."

I looked at Tony and Jerry and Finn, winced as I thought for the first time in months of my dead wife and child, killed years ago in a crash when the brakes I installed myself to save a buck failed in traffic. This was the place for absolution, all right—it was Callahan's stock in trade. And this seemed like our greatest challenge.

The brawny Irishman's voice shocked me when he spoke: it was as cold and hard as an axe-handle in February. "That word has another word in it," he said. "Solution. First let's find a solution, and then absolution will take care of itself. How can you stop this pogrom?"

Raksha's fur bristled; he looked flustered. "I cannot," he wailed.

"Can't you talk your people out of this?" Sam Thayer asked. "Won't they listen to you?"

"Impossible," the alien said flatly. "They could not conceivably understand my words . . . I am not sure I do myself. Have vegetarians made any real impact on your planet?"

"They have wherever they could convince folks that a cow might have a soul," the Doc asserted.

"But you *do not have the attribute*," Raksha insisted.

"I don't know what the hell this 'attribute' is," Callahan growled, "but I get the idea we have the potential for it; the symptoms, I believe you said. Could it be we never developed it because our people have been under the . . . protection of yours since our infancy?"

"No Krundai would believe that," Raksha replied. "If I voiced such an opinion, I would be judged insane and induced to suicide."

"Can you sabotage the campaign?" Telasco asked. "Join our side and do the guerrilla? With you to help we might . . ."

"No," Raksha said violently. "I cannot betray my people. It is unthinkable."

"It was unthinkable for me once," Tony persisted. "But when I saw what I had become, I repudiated what my people were doing, worked to stop it."

"Me too," Jerry chimed in.

"You do not understand," Raksha hissed. "You are *not-Krundai*—and this Finn may belong to a powerful, warlike race for all I know. I have committed an unthinkable crime by relying on your discretion and telling you all this—I can do no more."

Tony had a soldier's tactical mind. "Can you tell us where and how to locate your people? *We'll* stop them."

Finn spoke up before Raksha could answer. "That is not . . ."

"Possible," Callahan finished quickly, and I got the funny idea he'd kicked Finn's shin under the table. "If these boys led us by the hand to the atom bomb, there ain't a lot we can do to stop 'em, Tony."

"But . . . ouch," said Finn, and shut up.

"No," Callahan went on, "if anyone can help us, Raksha, it's you. Or did you just fall by to make a headsman's apology?"

"I can do nothing for you," Raksha said miserably. "I seek only absolution."

"Brother," I said sympathetically, "you're caught between a falling rock and a hard place." Sam and the Doc also began to make noises of commiseration, and Bill Gerrity started to ask Raksha what he was drinking. Just the men of Callahan's, offering understanding and help, as always.

But Callahan raised a hand. "No," he said quietly.

We stared at him, stunned. *Callahan* withholding absolution?

"You can't drink in my bar, brother," he said, staring Raksha in the eye, "and you can't have our forgiveness. There's a price for absolution on this planet, and it's called penance. Tony here gets arrested for joining demonstrations; Jerry has chucked away a pot-full of money he was making in real estate and started lobbying for green-belts and cluster housing; Finn here exiled himself among a lot of obnoxious, smelly humans for the sake of the ones worth saving. Buddhist monks who couldn't influence their governments any other way set themselves on *fire*, by Christ, and for their souls I pray on Sunday. What do *you* figure to do for atonement?"

Raksha closed his eyes—they were double-nictitating—and knotted his brow. He was silent for a long time.

"There is nothing I can do," he said at last, his voice hollow and bleak.

"Then there is no absolution for you," Callahan said flatly, "here or anywhere. Get out o' my joint and don't come back."

Raksha's face fell, and for a timeless moment I thought he was going to cry, or whatever Krundai do that's like crying. But he got a hold of himself, nodded once, rose and left the bar, shouldering party-people aside as he went.

There was another silence when he had gone, and we all looked at Callahan. His jaw was set, and his eyes flashed, challenging us to criticize his judgment.

"Were . . . weren't you a little harsh on the guy, Mike?" Doc Webster asked after a while.

"Hell, Doc," Callahan exploded, "that clown was Adolph Hitler! You want me to pat him on the head and say *it's all right, you were only following orders?* Christ on a minibike, if it wasn't for him and his kind, I might not have to run this goddamned bar. And my bunions give me the dickens."

"I grieve for him," Finn said tonelessly. "I too was once in a similar position."

"Save your grief, Finn," Callahan spat. "You had the same choice, but you followed through. And you weren't gutless—you were *counterprogrammed.* If you could figure out a way around the sheer physical limitations of your machinery, why the hell couldn't he overcome his conditioning? Conditioning isn't an excuse, for Krundai any more than for humans—it's an explanation. Thanks to you and the work you're doing, the Gaspé Peninsula may be prosperous farmland some day. You're still paying your dues. But that guy didn't want to atone, just apologize. He and his kind made this sorry old world what it is today, and maybe I could forgive that. But I don't give absolution free. It costs, costs you right in the old will power, and he wasn't willing to ante up. Fuck him, and the horse he rode in on."

"I still think we should have jollied him along and tried to pump him, Mike," Tony said insistently. "How are we going to find them to stop them now?"

Callahan looked tired. "As Finn started to say before I tromped on his toes, that ain't necessary. Now Finn knows they're here, he can find 'em for us as easy as you could spot a wolf in a chicken coop. That wasn't the prob . . ."

There came a shattering roar from outside. The building rocked; glass sprayed inward from the windows and bottles danced behind the bar. Everyone began to shout at once, and most of the boys made a bee-line for the door.

Only Callahan of all of us failed to jump. "Like I said, no guts," he said softly.

He rose quietly, walked through the suddenly-uncrowded bar the chalk line before the fireplace, picking up someone's drink as he went. He looked surreally absurd in that damned bear-suit he still had on, balding red head sticking out the top like a partially digested meal. He stood gazing into the flames for a moment, gulped the raw liquor and spoke in a clear, resonant baritone.

"To cowardice," he said, and flung the empty glass against the back wall of the fireplace with a savageness I had never seen in him before.

Fast Eddie stuck his head in the door. "Jeezis Christ, boss, de whole unprintable parkin' lot blew up."

"I know, Eddie," Callahan said gently. "Thanks. Anybody hurt?"

Eddie scratched his head. "I don't t'ink so," he allowed, "but dere's a lotta dead cars."

"Least of my worries," Callahan assured him. "Call the cops, will you? Tell 'em whatever you like." Eddie got busy on the phone.

Callahan came back to our table, stood over Finn. "Well, buddy, what do you say? Can you take 'em?"

Finn looked up at him for a while, figuring some things.

"That blast was powerful, Michael. They must have strong defenses."

"That's why I stepped on your toes and let that joker go, Mickey. If you two tangled in here, we'd have lost a lot more'n a few cars we can't gas anyway. But you heard what he said about violence."

"They abhor it," Finn agreed. "Even if they will employ it in self-defense, they are unused to it. Michael, I can take them. I will."

He rose and left the bar.

"Thanks, Mickey," Callahan called after him. I reckon your dues are paid in full."

There's been a lot of noise in the papers lately about the series of seismic shocks that have been recorded over the past few weeks in the unlikeliest places. An unpredicted miniquake every day or two for three weeks, culminating in a blockbuster where no quake had a right to be, is bound to cause talk.

The seismologist confess themselves baffled. Some note that none of the quakes took place in a densely populated area, and are reassured. Some note the uniquely powerful though strictly local intensity of the shocks, and are perturbed. Some note the utter inability of their science to explain the quakes even after the fact, and fear the end of the world is at hand.

But me and some of the boys at Callahan's Place suspect it's more like the beginning.

9

The Wonderful Conspiracy

I used to think that almost anything could happen at Callahan's Place. It wasn't long before I realized the truth: that anything can happen at Callahan's Place . . . and not long after that it was made clear to me that *anything* can happen at Callahan's.

But I confess I was still surprised the night I learned that A*N*Y*T*H*I*N*G can happen at Callahan's Place —and that, sooner or later, it probably will.

It was New Year's Eve, a natural time for introspection I guess. The Place was virtually empty, for the first time in a long while. Now that might strike you as downright implausible, but it's just another one of the inexplicable eccentricities of Callahan's that stop startling you after you've been hanging out there awhile. You see, the kind of guys that come in there regularly, if they've got families, tend to spend holidays with 'em at home.

It's that kind of crowd.

There are, of course, a handful who don't have families, and aren't willing to settle for the surrogate of a date, so Callahan stays open on holidays—but I'm sure he runs a net loss. This particular New Year's Eve, the entire congregation consisted of him, me, Fast Eddie, the Doc and Long-Drink McGonnigle.

Funny. You take men who already consider themselves deep and true friends: they've been drinking together regularly for many years, have experienced some memorable moments in each other's company, have given each other an awful lot. And yet somehow, on a night when there's just a few of them, there because they have no better place to be, such men can find an even deeper level of sharing; can, perhaps, truly become brothers. At such times they relax the shoulders of their souls, and turn their collective attention to those profound questions that can overawe a man alone. They bring out their utterly true selves. We shared a rich plane of awareness that night, Callahan behind the bar and the rest of us sitting together in front of it, lost in the glow of that special kind of intimacy that drink and good company bring, looking back over the year gone by and talking of nothing in general and everything in particular. What we were doing, we were telling dumb puns.

It started when Callahan taped over the cash-box a hand-lettered sign that read, "the buck stops *here*."

"Oh boy," rumbled the Doc, "I can see there'll be no quarter given tonight."—which is a pun because he chucked his glass into the fireplace as he said it, which meant the cigar-box at the end of the bar held at least two quarters that *he* wouldn't be given tonight.

Long-Drink got up and walked to the chalk line, and I assumed he wanted to give Doc's stinker the honor of a formal throw. I should have known he was setting us up. He toed the mark, announced, "To the poor corpuscle," drained his glass, and waited.

The Doc had reflexively drained the fresh glass Callahan had already supplied unasked—Doc will drink to *any*thing, sight unseen—but he paused with his arm in midthrow. "Wait a minute," he said. "Why the hell should I drink to 'the poor corpuscle'?"

"He labors in vein," Long-Drink said simply.

"Ah yes," I said without missing a beat, "but he vessles vhile he vorks."

"Plasma soul," exlaimed Callahan.

The Doc's eyes got round and his jaw hung down. "By god," he said at last, "I've never been outpunned by you rummies yet, and I'm not about to go down on *medical* puns. As a doctor I happen to know for certain there's only one other blood pun—I got it straight from the Auricle of Delphi."

There was an extended pause, and I was saying to myself, yep, as usual, no one can top the Doc—when all of a sudden Fast Eddie spoke up. Now you have to understand that while he's a genius at the piano, lightning wit has never been Eddie's strong suit; I don't think I'd ever heard him attempt a pun in the presence of so many masters.

But he by God opened his mouth and said with the nearest thing to a straight face he owns, "Well I dunno about youse guys, but anemia drink."

And even *then* he was not done, because while the Doc spluttered and the rest of us roared, Callahan quietly went into the gag that—unknown to us—Eddie had worked out with him before the rest of us arrived. Instead of Eddie's usual shot, the barkeep *mixed* him a drink, and served it with a wooden *chopstick* jutting out of the glass.

"What the hell kind of a drink is that?" Doc Webster demanded grumpily. And Eddie delivered it magnificently.

"A hickory dacquiri, Doc."

And the laughter of a mere three of us nearly blew out the windows.

The Doc was a good sport about it. In fact, he laughed so hard at himself that he lost three shirt buttons. But you could tell he was severely shaken: he paid for the next round. I felt as though I'd just seen a bulldozer to a dance myself. *The world is full of surprises*, I told myself.

Callahan put it even more succinctly. "It's a miracle,"

he whooped, setting up fresh glasses. ''A genuine damn miracle.''

Long-Drink snorted. ''Miracles are a dime a dozen in this joint.''

''You know, Drink,'' I said suddenly, ''you said a mouthful.''

''Hah?''

''Miracles. That's Mike's stock-in-trade. This is the place where nothing is impossible.''

''Horse feathers,'' Callahan said.

''No, I'm serious, Mike. I can think of half a dozen things that've happened in here in the past year that I wouldn't have believed for a minute if they'd happened anywhere else.''

''*That's* sure true enough,'' the Doc said thoughtfully. ''Little green men . . . *two* time travelers . . . Adolph Hitler . . .''

''That's not exactly what I mean, Doc,'' I interrupted. ''Those things're highly improbable, but if they could happen here, they could happen anywhere. What I mean is that, barring Raksha, every one of those jokers that walked in cryin' walked out smilin'—and even *he* could have, if he'd been willing to pay the freight. By me, that's a miracle.''

''I don't getcha,'' said Eddie, wrinkling up his face. Even more, I mean.

''Take that business of Jim and Paul MacDonald. Near as I can see, they represent the basic miracle of Callahan's Place, the greatest lesson this joint has taught us.''

''What's dat?''

''That there's nothing in the human heart or mind, no place no matter how twisted or secret, that can't be endured—if you have someone to share it with. That's what this place is all about: helping people to open up whatever cabinets in their heads hold their most dangerous secrets, and let 'em out. If you've got a hurt and I've got a hurt and we share 'em, some-crazy-how or other we each end up with less than half a hurt apiece.'' I took a sip of Bushmill's. ''That's what Callahan's Place has to offer—and as far as I know, there's no place like it in all the world.''

''I know one place kinda like it,'' Long-Drink said suddenly.

''What? Where?''

''Oh, I don't know that you'd spot the resemblance right off—*I* sure didn't. But did any o' you guys ever hear of The Farm?''

''I was raised on one,'' the Doc said.

''We know—in the barn,'' Long-Drink said drily. ''I ain't talking' about *a* farm. I mean *The* Farm—place down in Tennessee. Better'n eight hundred people livin' on a couple o' thousand acres. One of 'em's my daughter Anne, an' I went down to visit her last month.''

''One of them communes?'' the Doc asked skeptically.

''Not like I ever heard of,'' Long-Drink told him. ''They ain't got no house brand o' religion, for one thing—Anne still goes to Mass on Sundays. For another thing, them folks *work*. They feed themselves, an' they build their own houses, an' they take care of business. The heaviest drug I saw down there was pot, and they wasn't using that for recreation—said it was a sacrament.''

''Tennessee,'' I said, and whistled. ''They must get a hard time from the locals.''

''Not on your tintype. The locals love 'em. I spoke with the Lewis County sheriff, and he said if everybody was as decent and truthful and hard-working as the Farm folk, he'd be out of a job. I tell you, I went down there loaded for bear, ready to argue Annie into givin' up her foolishness and comin' on home. Instead I almost forgot to leave.''

''So what's all that got to do with this joint?'' Callahan asked.

''Well, it's like Jake was sayin' about sharing, Mike. Them folks share everything they got, an' the only rule I noticed was that a body that was hurtin' some way was everybody's number one priority. They . . .'' He paused, looked thoughtful. ''They *care* about each other. Eight hundred people, and they *care* about each other —and the whole damn world, too. That kind of thing's been out of style since Flower Power wilted.''

''Aw nuts,'' the Doc exclaimed. ''Another one of them fool nut cults is what it sounds like to me. They never last.''

''I dunno,'' Long Drink disagreed. ''They been goin' for about five years now, and they just started setting up colonies, like: ''Satellite Farms'' they call 'em, better'n half a dozen, all over the country.'' He paused, looking thoughtful. ''What got me, though, was how little attention they paid to their physical growth. That just seemed to happen by itself, while they put their real attention on the Main Game: gettin' straight with each other, so's they could live together. Seems to me like the whole world oughta be doin' that. Seems like if you be a better person, you have you a better life. Seemed to me like The Farm was Callahan's Place for hippies.''

''You're crazy,'' the Doc burst out. ''Sure, there's a thousand ham-headed gurus creepin' out from under every burning bush these days. The old-time religion went into the drink, so they're scratching for a new one like hungry hens, goin' in for mysticism and the occult and astrology and the late God only knows what-all. But I'm *damned* if I see the resemblance between a Jesus-freak revival meeting and this here bar.''

''Doc, Doc,'' I said softly, ''Slow down a bit. Yes, they're mass-producing religions like popcorn these days, and some of them are as plain silly as the sixteen-year-old perfect goombah with his divine Maserati and his sacred ulcer. But that don't make 'em *all* crazy. The point is that all them con-men must be filling *some* kind of powerful need, or they'd be working some more profitable grift. And I think I agree with Long-Drink: the need they're filling is the same one that brings folks to Callahan's Place.''

"Hmmph," the Doc snorted. ''And what need is that, pray tell?''

"It's pretty easy to see. For the last century or two we turned our attention to the physical world, to mastering the material plane at the expense of anything else. A lot of that, I'm compelled to believe, had to do with Raksha and his kind, but the tendency was there to exploit. And so we've got a world in which physical miracles are commonplace—and nobody's happy. We got what it takes to feed the whole three billion of us—and half of us are starving. You can show a dozen guys murderin' each other on TV but you can't ever show two people making love. A naked blade is reckoned to be less obscene than a naked woman. Ain't it about time we started trying to get a handle on love, *from any and all directions?*

"I don't know how come this Farm doesn't collapse like all the other communes. I don't know how come a government with the best propaganda machine ever built failed to sell a war to a country, for the first time in history. I don't know how come three or four guys managed to pull down a corrupt thug of a president. I don't even understand how come all the things this here bar stands for haven't been drowned under a sea of the drunks and brawlers and hookers and hoodlums every other bar gets, why the only people that seem to come here are the ones that need to, that ought to, that have to. *That's* the real miracle of this joint, you know, not our telepaths and little green men!

"I can't explain any of this stuff, Doc, but couldn't it be that there's some kind of new force loose on the world, like a collective-unconscious response to Raksha and the

Krundai, a new kind of energy that's trying to put us all back on the right track before it's too late? Couldn't it be that, now we've climbed out on a material-plane limb and started sawing at it, some mysterious force is trying to teach us how to fly? Whether it's our own stupidity or Krundai manipulation, we've stumbled across things that make a cobalt bomb look harmless: the human race is an idiot child in an arsenal. Couldn't it possibly be that under all these pressures, we're *beginning* to grow up?''

"Dat's what I loined from Rachel," Fast Eddie spoke up suddenly, startling me—I was so wrapped up in my own eloquence, I'd even forgotten my customary drawl and folksy speech-patterns.

"What do you mean, Eddie?" Callahan asked.

"Everybody's got roots in de past," Eddie explained. "But dey's got roots in de future too."

There was an awed silence. "I'll be damned," Callahan said after awhile. "That's twice in one night you've surprised me, Eddie. I never thought there was anything but music in that head o' yours. Guess even I can learn something in this joint." He shook his head and poured himself another shot.

Long-Drink tried to lighten the mood some. "I'll teach you something, Mike. What do you get when you put milk of magnesia in a glass of vodka?"

The Doc made a face. "Everybody knows that one: a Phillips screwdriver. The hell with that stuff: I want to hear more about this 'collective-unconscious' jazz."

Long-Drink grinned. "Sounds like this place to a T."

"Can it, I said. That 'mysterious force' stuff you were talkin' about, Jake—did you mean that literally?"

I thought about it. "You mean like a gang of sixth-column missionaries, Doc? A bunch of guys working undercover like Raksha an' his friends, only in reverse? No, I don't really think that's the way of it . . . *wups!*"

Reaching for my glass without looking, I knocked it

skittering across the bar, and leaped to grab it before it could fall into Callahan's lap. I froze for a moment, leaning half-over the bar—but I've always rather prided myself in being quick on the uptake.

". . . on the other hand," I continued calmly, "maybe that's exactly right. Who knows?"

And Callahan—who was still sitting as I had seen him, his legs folded under him in the full lotus, suspended a good three feet off the floor—winked, poured my glass brimfull of Bushmill's, and grinned.

"Not me," he lied, and puffed on his cigar.

"Hey youse guys," cried Eddie, eyes on the clock above us, "Happy New Year!"

BESTSELLING
Science Fiction
and
Fantasy